The True Diary Of That Girl

J.S. Cooper

This book is a work of fiction. Names, characters, places, and incidents either are the product of the author's imagination or are used fictitiously. Any resemblance to actual persons, living or dead, events, or locales is entirely coincidental.

The True Diary Of That Girl

J.S. Cooper

PROLOGUE

Life isn't easy. Love isn't easy. Fairy tales are books we read to children. Romance novels are books that make teenagers dream of love and happily ever afters. I'm here to tell you my story. This is my diary. This is my life. This is my truth. You can't make this shit up.

CHAPTER ONE

I'm not going to say my name, just in case this diary is found by someone. You can just call me 'that girl' like everyone else in my life. Well, not everyone else, but a lot of people in my town. When I was younger, I was the girl everyone felt sorry for. Now, I'm just the girl everyone whispers about in the streets. Only they don't even know me. My best friend, Natasha, thinks it's ironic that so many women judge me and think they're better than I am. If they only knew the real me, they wouldn't be smirking quite so much.

First off, you should know that I don't care about anyone other than my best friend, Natasha, my other best friend, Tom, and my dog, Lulu the Great (even though she's not that great). You might be surprised to hear that I have a boyfriend. A very handsome and very rich boyfriend. He pays for my apartment. A luxury apartment in the city. It costs about $4,000 a month in rent. I know that because I get a kickback of $2,000 a month from the landlord. Don't ask me why or how. We don't know each other well enough for me to be divulging all my secrets.

I suppose you want to know my boyfriend's name? I can give you his first name, but if I give you his last name as well, you may figure out who he is. And I can't have that.

Aiden is his name. Yes, like Aiden from *Sex and the City*, a show I loved. I always thought Carrie should have chosen Aiden as opposed to Mr. Big, but what do I know? I'm not really an expert in love. Aiden is thirty-three, and he has short, dark-brown hair and green eyes. I think he's Irish-Italian, with his name coming from his Irish roots and his naturally tan skin coming from his Italian side. He calls it olive skin; I say tan. Olives are green and black. He's neither of those.

I told you before that he's hot, right? He looks like Tom Cruise's taller and handsomer brother. The other plus is that he's good in bed. And when I say good, I mean flip-me-over-and-do-me-again good. I never have to say no to him. I should say I never *want* to say no to him. It would be a perfect relationship—if things were different.

Natasha thinks that Aiden is a jerk, and Tom thinks that he's not good enough for me. They're both right, of course, but I don't care. I get what I want from him. Even if it's not a love connection. I don't really believe in true love. I mean, how can one man and one woman fall in love and spend the rest of their lives together? I've never seen it work. Not once. I don't know any happily married couples.

Natasha thinks I'm jaded. I know, I know. I talk about Natasha a lot. She's important to me. She's what

I call a true friend. She's one of those friends who makes you feel like you've won something in life. She's the real deal: genuine, compassionate, non-judgmental, and always there for me.

Most people would assume that she is some loser to put up with me. But Natasha is probably the best person you could ever meet. She's beautiful, as in Hollywood beautiful, with long, blond hair, blue-green eyes, a tiny waist, and a sweet smile. She's also brilliantly smart. She has a college degree from an Ivy League university and works as a pharmacist at a local drugstore. She's also married to her college boyfriend, Brad. I don't like him very much, so I'm not going to dwell on him.

Natasha and I are both twenty-five. We've been friends since preschool and she's never dropped or judged me. Not even when she went to her fancy school and I went somewhere else. We talk every day and she knows everything about me. Well, almost everything.

Tom is my other best friend. He's that guy every girl should have in their lives. He can fix things and be a listening ear when I need one. He gives me the male perspective whenever I need one. Oh, and he used to be my lover. Well, not just used to. We're still friends with benefits. But that's between us.

That's one of the things Natasha doesn't know. It's not like it's every week or even every month. Just sometimes when I need someone to hold me. I call him and he comes over. And his coming over usually leads to sex. Hot, passionate, no-holds-barred sex.

Don't judge me. I know it looks bad that I have my friend come over and fuck me in the apartment my boyfriend pays for. I never said I was a good girl. I don't think you could go through the things I have in life and be a good girl.

Tom's handsome as well, with his black hair and hazel eyes. He's not very successful, though. He's a writer. And I guess writing doesn't pay that well. But he loves it and I suppose that's all that matters. To him, anyways. I could never be with a guy who couldn't afford me the finer things in life. What can I say? I've done poor. I don't want to do it again.

And then there's me. I already told you that I won't tell you my name. But you can know what I look like. I'm above average height, about five eight to be exact. I'm slender, with long, black hair, big, brown eyes, and voluptuous boobs that may or may not be natural. I'm what men call an exotic beauty. I don't know why, exactly. I'm not from anywhere special. I grew up in the Midwest. But I suppose what a handsome man wants to call you is his business. If they have money and are good in bed, I don't care.

I suppose you think I'm a slut? I'm not, but I've heard that before. Usually from jealous women. But what can I say? I love sex. Is there any other activity that can make your body shudder with the most exquisite pleasure known to mankind for free? I think not. Sex is like free chocolate every day of your life that doesn't make you fat. In fact, it makes you skinnier. How cool is that?

Wow, I've been really talkative today. Usually I like to keep to myself, but today I'm feeling like putting it all out there. Sometimes I think my life is a Lifetime movie. I mean, that's how it feels. Like my first lover—let me tell you more about him.

The first time I had sex, I was eighteen years old and a senior in high school. His name was Andrew. I wasn't always a good student in high school and my grades reflected that even though I never failed a class. However, I nearly failed chemistry. I just didn't understand or care. How was I supposed to remember the periodic table? Hydrogen, helium, lithium—say what? Neutrons, electrons, atoms. I mean, really? When the teacher started saying that the air was made up of tiny atoms, he lost me. I couldn't see shit, and if I can't see it, I don't believe it.

So, one afternoon, the teacher told me to wait after school. He said, "You're going to fail this class and you're going to have to repeat it." Which meant I wouldn't graduate on time. I thought my world was about to end.

This is the point where I'm guessing you think I'm going to say that Andrew was a cute boy in my class and he offered to tutor me and I ended up getting an A. If this was a cutesy piece of fiction, that's most probably how this story would go. However, this is my life, and as you should know by now, my life isn't cutesy. I did end up getting an A in the class and I did graduate on time, but that was because Andrew was my teacher and I gave him an offer he couldn't refuse.

The Offer

"Mr. Matthews, can I speak to you after class?" I asked him, batting my eyelashes.

"Sure." He glanced at me with a stern expression.

"Thank you." I smiled back with my most seductive expression and spread my legs slowly.

Andrew's eyes widened as he realized I didn't have any panties on under my skirt.

"No problem." His face looked flushed as he looked away.

I grinned to myself as I saw him peeking at me every couple of minutes. He stumbled and bumbled through class, and he was positively squirming when the bell rang.

"How can I help you, Ms. X?" he asked me once everyone had left the room.

"I'm having trouble understanding the assignments, Mr. Matthews." I walked to his desk, swinging my hips slowly and pushing my breasts out. I heard him gasp as he realized that he could see my nipples through my white top. I'd pulled my bra off and put it in my bag as the other students exited the room.

"How can I help you understand?"

"I don't know if I'm ever going to get it!" I pouted and walked over to stand next to him. "I just feel like I'm never going to be good at chemistry." I brushed my chest against his arms, and he jumped back.

"Maybe you can get a tutor?" He looked at me warily.

"Would you be my tutor?" I gazed up at him with wide eyes. "Please?"

"I don't know." He gazed down at me and swallowed hard.

"Please, Mr. Matthews." I grabbed his hand then and brought it up to my right breast. His eyes widened as he realized what I was doing. "I think we'd both benefit from you being my tutor."

He stood there for a second and mumbled something before pulling his hand away.

"There are many things I want you to teach me, Andrew." I breathed softly and tried again.

This time, I grabbed his hand and lifted my skirt up. I placed his hand in between my legs and rubbed his fingers gently across my wetness. He breathed in sharply and his eyes widened.

"What are you doing?" he asked me sharply, but he didn't remove his fingers away.

"I just want to pass the class, Mr. Matthews." I licked my lips slowly and closed my legs together.

"I don't know what you expect me to do." He stared back at me with confusion in his face. I knew that he had mixed emotions about what was going on.

"I think you do." I leaned up and kissed him. "I think you do."

"Shit." He groaned, and I felt one of his fingers entering me.

I grinned against his mouth then. That was when I knew I had won. I was going to graduate and I didn't have to worry about my stupid chemistry class anymore.

I suppose you think that what I did was cheap and wrong. But you're the one who's wrong. Andrew was a great first lover, and it was exhilarating finding new ways to have sex in school. If you only knew half of the things we did. We even had sex during class one day. I'm sure you're trying to figure out how that happened. Maybe one day I'll tell you.

However, this diary isn't about Andrew and our crazy sexual adventure. This diary is about me and my crazy life. It's about all the things I did that I can't deny. It's not pretty, but it's all true. Aside from one thing. I lied about Aiden's age. He's not thirty-three. He's a bit older than that. But that didn't matter to me.

Not until that one day. Because that one day, I met a guy who seemed to see right through my soul. His name was Dominic. And Dominic was to be the undoing of me. You see, he was to become the first man I fell in love with. Only, falling in love doesn't always mean rainbows and butterflies. This is the true story of my life and how love changed everything!

CHAPTER TWO

If you didn't already realize it, I like to have fun. Clean fun, dirty fun—I don't care. I figure I might as well live my life to the fullest. That's one thing Aiden likes about me. I'm not all over him like some desperate whore. And yeah, I said 'likes' and not 'loves.' I'm pretty sure Aiden doesn't love me. Well, aside from every Saturday night when I say yes to whatever he wants to do. And he likes to do a lot.

Last weekend, he brought over a gag. It was different. I can't say that it was my favorite. I'm not really a BDSM girl, but I do what he wants. He knows better than to whip me, though I'm always down for a good spanking. Some of my best orgasms have been after he's spanked me. I actually have a pretty good story about one of the hottest times he spanked me. I'll tell you if you promise not to judge me. I've already told you that I'm not a good girl.

The Best Spanking of My Life

"Tom, you have to leave." I tried pushing him through the door. "Now is not a good time."

"But I need some of your sweet loving." He grinned as his fingers found my butt and pushed me towards him.

"Not tonight." I shook my head. "Come over tomorrow."

"Tomorrow's Sunday. You know that I like to go to Central Park and write on Sundays."

"Then come over on Monday."

"I don't want to." He leaned forward and kissed me.

Once his lips hit mine again, I couldn't resist. Tom always tasted like home. I'm not sure why, but once he kissed me, I was putty in his hands.

"Tom," I groaned as he lifted my top up. "What are you doing?"

"I'm undressing you." He laughed as he quickly peeled my bra off. "So that I can make sweet love to you."

"It's not a good time." I shook my head but found my fingers reaching for his pants. "Tom," I groaned again as I felt his hard erection. "You have ten minutes."

"Shh." He picked me up and carried me to the bed before quickly pulling my panties and skirt off.

"Oh." I moaned as he bent down and started licking my pussy.

His tongue traced circles as his lips sucked on my clit. I could feel my body trembling as his fingers reached up and pinched my nipples.

"Fuck!" I screamed as his tongue slowly entered me. I could feel my wetness on his face as his tongue slowly teased me.

DING DONG.

I froze when the doorbell rang. I looked at the clock and sighed. Aiden was fifteen minutes early.

"You have to go in the closet!" I jumped up and pushed Tom.

He gave me a look and frowned. "What the fuck?"

"I told you you had to leave." I pushed him in. "Aiden's here."

"Fuck," he groaned, and I nodded. Tom knew that Aiden was my boyfriend and the reason I was able to live in this apartment.

"Just keep quiet." I quickly grabbed my robe and ran to open the front door.

"What took you so long?" Aiden walked into the living room and stared at me before slowly smiling as he took in my appearance. "Getting ready for me, were you?"

"Perhaps." I laughed, and I gasped as he pushed aside my gown and shoved his fingers in between my legs.

"I'd say yes." His fingers stroked my wetness before he pulled them out and sucked them while staring in my eyes. "I'd say you were more than getting yourself ready for me. You were trying to get yourself off."

"What can I say? I was horny." I raised an eyebrow at him, and he shook his head before kissing me hard.

I kissed him back and played with his hair, laughing to myself inside. That was the problem with powerful men like Aiden. They never thought that a woman would have the gumption to cheat on them, even though they cheated all the time. There was no doubt in his mind that I'd just been in the bedroom playing with myself. He had no clue that another man had just been going down on me. That another man was currently hiding in the closet as we spoke. It made me feel heady with power, and I shivered as I thought about how kinky the whole thing was. I told you—I'm fucked up.

"You've been a naughty girl. You need a spanking." He walked me to the couch, but I shook my head.

"Let's go to the bedroom and you can teach me a lesson there." I grabbed his hand and escorted him to my room. I was oddly turned on by the fact that Tom was about to watch me with Aiden and Aiden didn't even know.

"You love being a naughty girl, don't you?" Aiden grabbed me by the waist and swung me around. "You like it when my hand smacks your ass."

"Oh yes. Spank me!" I squealed.

This was indeed true. I did like it when he spanked me. He was never too hard, but he was hard enough that, when he rubbed me after a slap, it felt good. I wasn't into hard, tortuous pain, but I wasn't going to say no to some nerve endings being heightened.

I ran away from Aiden and into the bedroom, and he caught up with me and pushed me onto the bed.

"You're a bad girl." His voice was deep as he stared down at me longingly.

I knew he was ready to fuck, and that was what I loved about being with him. Even though he was older, he was always able to get it up. I didn't know if he was on Viagra or not, but he always had a hard one ready to go.

"You're a bad boy." I reached up and pulled him down towards me. "And that's why I want you to fuck me." I played with his hair and laughed. "You need to dye it again. I'm seeing grey." I played with his locks, and he frowned.

Aiden hated being reminded of his own mortality and age. I know, I know—you want to know. How old is he really? I know I told you that he was thirty-three before. I didn't want to shock you, but I think we're past that now. Aiden is fifty. Did your jaw drop? Don't knock fifty until you've been with a man like Aiden. He doesn't look a day over forty and he's got more energy than men half his age.

Aiden took me over his knee then, and I felt his hand hard against my butt as he spanked me. "That's for saying I'm going grey," he muttered and spanked me again.

I wiggled on his lap and groaned as I felt his fingers gently rub against me as he caressed my stinging ass. I heard a small gasp and knew that Tom could see everything. I opened my legs slightly to give him a better view.

"Are you enjoying this?" He spanked me again, and I closed my eyes as he continued with his foreplay.

"Yes, sir. No, sir. Three bags full, sir."

"Impertinent little..." he growled, and I jumped up and pushed him back down on the bed.

"Impertinent little what?" I whispered as I quickly unzipped his pants.

His cock stood to attention as my mouth descended on him. I licked along his shaft and played with his balls, and I could feel his breathing growing heavy.

"Fuck. You know just how to turn me on." He groaned as I continued to take him deep into my mouth.

"That's why we're so good together." I laughed and then moaned as he flipped me onto my back. He jumped up, flipped me over and I felt his hand rubbing my ass before smacking it again.

"You don't suck me until I say you can." He grunted at me, and I lay there smiling into the bed.

I thought it was funny when he tried to act dominant. Part of Aiden's midlife crisis was his deciding to take on the role of an alpha male. Not that I minded. I liked it when a man took control.

"Uh huh," I whispered into the sheets. Then I groaned as I felt him smack me again and then slip two fingers into me.

I came as soon as his fingers entered me. I was already worked up from Tom's tongue, and now Aiden had pushed me over the edge. Knowing that Tom was witnessing everything was the icing on the cake. I've often wondered why that was such a turn-on and I don't know why. Tom and I have never discussed it. I mean, who was he to say anything to me? He wasn't my boyfriend. And while Aiden was, it wasn't like I was his one and only. Shit, to Aiden, I was a sexy plaything. Someone who gave him pleasure. And I was happy to be that person to him. Like I said before, I didn't do love.

***

"Tell me three things you like about Aiden." Natasha sat back smugly and grinned.

"He's hot, he's good in bed, and he has money. Lots of money." I sipped on my Tequila Sunrise and grinned back at her. "He's the reason why we're sitting in the Red Lounge right now in a booth."

I gestured to all the other girls who were dancing by the booths, hoping that some rich man would invite them to sit down. They were living the sucker's life. I was no sucker. I wasn't going to go to an exclusive club and hope that a man would see my beauty and deign to make me a VIP for the night. Only dumb girls did that.

Natasha looked back at me, unblinking. "Tell me three things that aren't superficial." That was what I liked about Natasha—she didn't play nice or dumb. She cut straight to the point. It was funny how stuff like that worked. She saw everything around her clearly—except for what her husband, Brad, was truly like. She had blinders on where he was concerned.

"You think that it's superficial that he's like dynamite in bed?" I raised an eyebrow at her, and she rolled her eyes.

At this point, you would think that she would get the hint. I wasn't going to budge from my stance. I had never budged. It was always about sex for me. Love didn't exist to me. I thought that romantic love was a farce. I mean, lust was where it's at. How many men do you know who can keep it zipped up for fifty years married to one woman? I don't know any.

"Come on. Don't you want to fall in love?" She gave me one of her looks.

"No." I shook my head, answering honestly. It was true. I didn't care about falling in love. In fact, it was the one thing I dreaded most.

"Once you fall in love, you're going to realize that—"

"Natasha, I'm in love with Aiden's dick!" I said loudly. "Isn't that good enough?"

The people in the booths next to us looked at me as if I were a criminal just escaped from prison. I looked back at them and smiled sweetly. I didn't give a shit what they thought about me. Who were they?

"You're too much. You know that, right?"

"That's why you love me." I jumped up onto the table and started dancing to the pulsating music. It was loud and it was fast, but I moved my body slowly, gyrating my hips as I moved to the bottom of the table and back up.

As I danced, I noticed a guy standing next to the bar, staring at me. I closed my eyes, moved my hips even more sensuously, and shook my hair. I opened my eyes again and saw that the guy had moved to a position even closer to me and was watching me openly.

He was pretty cute. Maybe six feet tall, with bulging muscles and a thick head of straight, black hair that had been recently gelled. He looked like he was an Italian bonehead, but who was I to judge?

We made eye contact and he gave me a small nod and a smile. I turned away from him then and continued dancing. I looked down at Natasha and she was laughing at me. That was what I loved about her.

She was one of the girls who always had my back no matter what I did.

I pulled my top off then and threw it into her lap. Her eyes widened as I danced in my half-cup Victoria's Secret push-up bra. I felt my breasts bouncing as I danced and I grinned to myself. I could see about five other guys staring at me now, hoping for an accident. I reached up, grabbed my breasts, squeezed them as I danced, and closed my eyes.

It was only about a minute before the Italian stud walked up and grabbed me off the table.

"Hey, what are you doing, big boy?" I whispered up at him breathlessly.

And no, I wasn't breathless or taken away by him coming and grabbing me. I really wanted to say, "What took you so long?" but a lesson I've learned is that you have to make the man feel like he's in control. He needs to feel like he's the one making decisions. He chose me. He doesn't want to know that I'd spotted him from across the bar, jumped up on the table to turn him on with my dance, and sealed the deal by taking my shirt off and grabbing my breasts.

Let's be real—grabbing my own breasts does nothing for me. I clean them every fucking day in the shower. You think I wanna orgasm every time I check them out? But that's part of the fantasy for men. They think that what they wanna do is what you wanna do.

"What's your name?" he growled into my ear as he carried me to the wall at the side of the bar.

I wrapped my legs around his waist as he carried me. I liked a strong man. I wasn't light as a feather either, so he had to be bench-pressing a good amount.

"Onlegs," I whispered, and he frowned.

"Sorry. Did you say onlegs?" he repeated, and I grinned.

"Yeah, I'm sex on legs."

"Sex on legs?" he repeated like a dummy for a minute. "Oh," he grinned as it dawned on him. "Nice to meet you, Ms. Sexy."

"You too, Rambo."

"Sorry, what?"

"You're Rambo for the night." I reached up and caressed his hair. "Every Italian stud is Rambo in my eyes."

"My name's Antonio."

I wanted to laugh in his face. As if I cared that his real name was Antonio. He was cute enough, but I could tell from his watch, shoes, and cologne that he wasn't a guy I needed in my life. I was pretty sure his whole outfit cost less than my bag.

"So, Rambo, what's the plan for the night?"

"Wanna go back to my place?"

"No." I made a face. I had a feeling that he was from the Bronx. And there was no way I was going back to the Bronx.

"We can go back to your place." He looked at me eagerly, probably figuring out that I didn't live in the Bronx and was getting excited about living it up for a night.

"Hell no." I shook my head.

"So what, then?" He looked annoyed, probably thinking that he'd carried me for nothing.

I could feel his hardness pressed up against me and I was pleasantly surprised by the size of him.

"Don't tell me you're just being a teasing bitch."

Okay, just so you know—no one calls me a bitch. It's one of those words that gets my juices burning. There was no way I was going to let Rambo get away with calling me a bitch, but I'm smart enough to not get angry right away. What does that serve? If I gave him a slap and walked away, he'd be like, "Stupid bitch," and move on. No, I was going to teach him a lesson.

"I'm not a tease." I giggled up at him and pressed my boobs against his chest while reaching down and grabbing him through his jeans.

His body went still with shock and pleasure. I know that I said earlier, "Don't show a guy that you can take charge," but that's while he's still pursuing you. Once you're with him, you should go in for the attack. Show him who's boss. Take what you want. Trust me, with most men, you'd better know what you like and how to get off or you're going to be suffering through some boring sex for a long time. 'In out, in out' doesn't get anyone off if he's not doing it right.

"So what you got planned if you don't wanna go to my place or your place?" he muttered, and I tried to hide my distaste.

At this point, any classy guy would say, "Let me take you to a hotel," and if it's the Ritz Carlton or Trump International, he's got a good chance of hearing me say yes.

"Who says we have to go anywhere?" I leaned up and kissed him. His lips were soft and tasted like gin—not my favorite taste, but it wouldn't make me puke.

"I like where you're going with this." He looked down into my eyes, and I felt his fingers fumbling around at the back of my bra.

His tongue entered my mouth as he finally got the bra undone, and I was pleasantly surprised that he was a good kisser even if his fingers weren't the deftest. He pushed me forward slightly and pulled up my bra. I shivered slightly as the cold air hit my skin but didn't hide my naked breasts from him or from the two guys who were standing next to us and gaping. I gave them a small smile as I pressed my breasts into Rambo's chest. I turned slightly to make sure Natasha was okay and I saw her laughing and texting on her phone.

"What are you doing?" Rambo frowned as I turned around.

"I want to dance." I started moving my ass against his crotch as his fingers reached up and grabbed my breasts gingerly.

I knew he wasn't prepared for this. It was okay for me to be dancing by myself in public, but I knew he felt uncomfortable with our public display. My naked breasts were bouncing for all the room to see and his fondling of them showed his discomfort. I grinned as I moved. I was taking all of the power away from him and he didn't even know it. I felt bad for Rambo. In all likelihood, I would have gone into the bathroom with him for a quickie, but he'd ruined that opportunity with one word. I was about to show him what a bitch could really do.

The guys next to me were entranced by us both now. I knew that it would only be minutes before everyone knew what was up and I was getting kicked out, so I got to work quickly.

"Hey, big boy. Why don't you show me what you're working with?" I turned around and fluttered my eyelashes at him.

"Working with?" He frowned again, and I realized that he was way too slow for me.

I kept the smile on my face and reached my hands down his pants. "How big is your cock?"

"Uh, I don't know." He shrugged, and I could see his face going red. *Pussy!*

"I'd say about seven inches, big boy." I squeezed him and ran my fingers down his girth.

"Uh—"

"Shh." I leaned forward and kissed him. I didn't think I'd be able to fake it for much longer. I unzipped his pants and pulled them down slightly.

"What are you doing?" He grabbed my hands to stop me.

"I want you to fuck me from behind."

"Here?" He looked around, and I could hear the panic in his voice.

"Why not?" I grinned and pressed my breasts against his chest again.

"Uh, I..." he started, and I just yanked his pants down.

His cock stood to attention, and I stood in front of him and started dancing again. He grabbed my breasts and then started to massage my butt. One of the guys next to us looked like he was going to faint in shock and I winked at him before quickly grabbing his drink. I took a sip and then slowly turned around before pouring the drink over Rambo's hard cock and pants.

"What the fuck?" He jumped back, angry.

"What?" I laughed, pulled my top back on, and grabbed my bra. "That's what us bitches do." I smiled sweetly at him and walked away, swinging my hips as I walked back to my booth. I collapsed next to Natasha and started laughing.

"Did you just fuck that guy?" she asked, not looking surprised.

"Nah, he missed out." I shook my head.

"You shouldn't be picking up strange guys in clubs."

"Yes, Mom." I rolled my eyes.

"You know that's not cool."

"Yawn." I fluttered my fingers in front of my mouth.

"I wish you would find a guy and settle down like me and Brad have."

"I don't want a Brad." I shivered as I thought about her husband.

"I want you to find love."

"I've got love." I grinned and hugged her to me. "I've got you."

"Is that your bra?" She looked down at my lap.

"Uh huh."

"Why don't you have your bra on?"

"I don't know." I grinned at her.

"You did fuck him." Her eyes widened, and I shook my head.

"Nope."

"Liar."

"I don't lie." At least I tried not to lie to Natasha. I figured that lies to your best friend weren't worth it.

"What am I going to do with you?" She shook her head and laughed as she stared at me.

"Buy me another drink." I grinned at her impishly.

"How about *I* buy you a drink?" A smooth voice interrupted our conversation, and I turned to see who had spoken. I was annoyed that a man had been listening to us talking and I hadn't known.

As I looked into the guy's blue-green eyes, I felt my heart stop for one brief second. There was a twinkle in his eyes and he had a devilish smile on his handsome face.

"I don't think so." I turned away from him and shook my head, trying to forget his handsome face.

"I don't bite," he said. "Unless you want me to."

"What?" I frowned and stared at him.

"I don't bite. What would you like to drink?"

"Nothing." I turned back to Natasha, who was grinning at me.

"I'm Dominic, by the way. In case you wanted to know."

"I don't," I muttered without turning back to him.

"What's your name?"

"Wouldn't you like to know?"

"That's why I asked," he continued, and I tried not to laugh.

That was the first time I met Dominic. I wish I could tell you that it was the day that I started to believe in love. I wish I could say that I turned around, accepted that drink, and rode into the sunset together. I wish I could tell you that it was the night where I suddenly realized that I could have the fairy tale. But it wasn't.

That was the night that the beginning of the end began. That was the night that started a chain of events that changed my life forever. Dominic was a catalyst in my life—that is true. He was the man who changed everything. He was the man who made me lose myself even more than I'd been lost. And I have no one to blame but myself.

CHAPTER THREE

I don't care about love. It means nothing to me. I've told you that already. Men, for the most part, can't be trusted. I know that. You know that. They know that. Do you know how many husbands I see at the club trying to get into my pants? As if I can't see the tan line on their finger from where they've taken their wedding ring off. It's shameful. Love is a charade. A charade that men go along with so that they can treat women like crap and get away with it.

I sound bitter, don't I? *What got in this bitch's bonnet?* is what you're thinking right now, right? Look, we're not friends and I don't care what you think of me, but I'm going to let you in on a little secret. I do care about love, just a little bit. It's not an everyday thing. I don't walk down the street looking for Mr. Right. I'm not online looking at rings, daydreaming of getting married on some white sand beach in St. Barths.

No, it hits me when I'm in bed late at night and I realize I'm all alone. Sometimes it hits me and I think, *Is this it?* That's a powerful moment. We've all experienced it at some point. "Is this my life?" It's scary. Not only because you realize you're not fulfilled, but also because you don't know what to do to fix it.

Sometimes I think, maybe a husband would provide me the security and the happiness I'm searching for. Maybe a man could fill that void. Then I think of all the problems that men bring with them and I know that's not it.

I know it's not a baby, either. Don't get me wrong, babies are cute, but I need my sleep. Long, deep hours of slumber are the only way I can survive.

That was until I met Dominic. He turned my every thought and emotion on its head.

The Day Dominic Found Out My Name

If you believe in things like fate—which I don't, by the way—you'll think that my meeting Dominic at the coffee shop about a week later was a sign that we were meant to be together. I mean, he's hot, I'm hot—what more could one want, right?

Everything seemed to go in slow motion that morning. I'd woken up feeling tired and uneasy. I'd rolled out of bed and pulled on a T-shirt and jeans without even thinking of makeup or underwear. I hadn't even brushed my hair, just scooped it up into a ponytail. For some reason, I just needed to get out of the apartment. I wanted fresh air and a hot cup of freshly brewed coffee.

Being that I'm not one of those girls into running every morning, I decided to go to the Starbucks at the corner of the street and not the gourmet coffee shop about three blocks away. What can I say? If I don't have to walk too far, I'm not going to. I ordered a white chocolate mocha. I know, I know. Who has a white chocolate mocha when they are in need of a coffee fix? Then I waited for my drink as patiently as possible.

I knew the minute he walked into the store. It was as if someone had reached out and pricked me with a pin. I felt a short, quick jab of pain. And then I saw him. His eyes looked surprised when he saw me. Surprised, but happy. He came over to me right away. I was taken aback by the hug he gave me.

"Imagine seeing you again."

"You'd think we lived in the same city or something." I raised an eyebrow at him, and he laughed.

"You look different."

"From what? Other human beings?"

"From the night I saw you at the club."

"Oh, because I have on clothes?"

"No, because you have on no makeup." He surveyed my face and smiled. "You're pretty without makeup."

"Should I say thank you now? Should I preen up at you and blink my eyelashes?"

"If you want." He grinned down at me, his aquamarine eyes shining, and I couldn't stop myself from smiling back at him. "So what's your name, Ms. Pretty With No Makeup On?"

"That's for me to know." I looked away from him, feeling slightly uncomfortable.

I'd never had it this easy and carefree before. I didn't like it. I needed to know why a man was into me. I needed to know what he wanted. I didn't know what he wanted.

"Want to sit together?"

I rolled my eyes at him. "You haven't even ordered as yet."

"I'll order, then we can sit and chat like two normal adults."

"I'm not normal."

"I've gathered that." His eyes crinkled, and I watched as he ran his hands through his damp, dark-brown hair.

"Are you saying I'm weird?" I frowned, and that's when it happened.

"Saskia!" the stupid barista shouted out and I froze. "Saskia."

"Is that your name?" He grinned at me. "I like that. I like Saskia."

And that was it. My secret was out. I guess you know, too, now. My name is Saskia. I'll keep my last name private. A girl's got to keep something to herself, right?

I wish I could tell you that what happened next was something from a movie. That we went and sat down and had coffee and fell in love, slowly but surely, reveling in the wonders of each other. That's not what happened.

Dominic went and got his drink, and I did wait for him. We sat down at a table, and within a few minutes, my right foot was out of my sandal and in his crotch, rubbing him gently. He didn't even look surprised. I'll give him that. I suppose when you're tall, hot, and loaded (I could tell he was loaded by his $20,000 Rolex and his $5,000 Italian leather shoes), women are all over you. He grabbed my foot as I continued caressing his growing hardness and started massaging it, caressing my arches and kneading my pressure points.

I saw a couple of people staring at us, but neither of us cared. They were just jealous. Who wouldn't want to get a foot massage in a Starbucks? Of course, it was all too comfortable and sweet. You should know that by now. So I leaned forward, grabbed his shirt, and pulled him towards me.

"Meet me in the bathroom in three minutes. The code is 34568. I'll leave it unlocked." I pulled my foot back, placed it back into my shoe, and stood up slowly, giving him a wide smile before slowly licking my lips and walking to the bathroom.

Now you should know that there are two kinds of girls that have casual sex. The ones who hope the casual sex becomes a relationship and the ones like me who don't give a fuck. We just want it hot and fast and we don't care if we ever hear from the guy again. Men don't get us. They expect all of us women to be clingy and hinting to see each other again, and the worst is when we go for declarations of love. When a woman is like a man and just takes what she wants, she makes the man uncomfortable. I love making men uncomfortable. And I very much wanted to make Dominic uncomfortable because he was making me feel things I'd never felt before.

***

"I'm here." He entered the bathroom, staring at me with wide eyes. I grinned at the shock in his expression. "What if someone else had entered?" He stared at my naked body in shock.

"Just shut up." I swiftly moved towards him and ran my fingers down his chest as I kissed him.

He passionately kissed me back and pushed me back into the sink. His fingers found my breasts and squeezed, gently playing with my nipples as he cupped them. I reached down to his pants and unzipped him, eagerly pulling his hard cock out. I moaned against him as I felt his fingers playing with my clit. I was already wet, and all I could think about was feeling him inside me.

He rubbed his cock against me and I closed my legs, hoping to feel him slide up inside me. This is what I liked about hot and quick fucks. There were no games. There was no playing around. You just got straight to the point.

"Not yet, Saskia." He laughed, turned me around, and slapped my ass a few times. "Like that, do you?"

"Shut up, you sadist." I laughed and bent over the sink. "Just fuck me."

"Okay." He grabbed my hips, pulled my ass back to him, and then quickly entered me. "Shit, you feel so good," he said, moaning as his cock slid in and out of me roughly.

I moaned in response to him and looked into the mirror in front of me. Our eyes met, and we both stared at the other as he continued to fuck me hard. I watched as my breasts jiggled against the sink and then as his fingers reached around to play with them.

"I'm nearly about to come." He grunted. "Are you?"

"No." I shook my head, and he moaned.

Then he reached his fingers down and started playing with my clit as he continued to fuck me. I immediately felt my walls tensing as my orgasm built up.

"Oh yeah!" I screamed as his cock slammed in and out of me while his fingers rubbed me furiously. "Just keep rubbing," I commanded him, not wanting him to stop either action.

"Fuck, I'm about to come!" he shouted, and I felt his body shuddering as he released inside me.

My body started trembling about twenty seconds later as his fingers brought me to orgasm as well.

"I'm coming!" I screamed loudly as our bodies shuddered together.

BANG BANG.

The door opened and a man in a Starbucks uniform walked in.

"What is going on in here?" He looked pissed, and I watched as he stared at us. I gave him a small grin and gyrated my hips against Dominic. "Get the fuck out of my store or I'll call the police."

"Yes, sir." I squeezed my breasts together as he stared at me. "Sorry."

"You have two minutes." His face was red, but his eyes never left my breasts.

I gave my nipples a quick squeeze for his benefit. "Sure." I laughed, and he walked out.

I pulled away from Dominic, quickly grabbed my clothes, and pulled them on. Dominic had a dazed expression on his face as if he couldn't understand what had just happened. I smiled to myself as I walked out of the bathroom with him following me. I felt like I was in charge again, and that was how I liked it.

***

"Will I see you again?" He looked at me casually as we quickly left the store, both of us grinning as the manager shouted.

"I don't think so." I shook my head and tried not to think about how good he had felt inside me.

"I'm going away next weekend." He made a face. "Family get-together, even though Dad is bringing work home with him."

"I don't care." I shrugged and looked away.

"But maybe we can get together the weekend after that?"

"No." I sighed and looked at him. "Thanks for the fuck, but I'm not interested. I don't want to date. I don't want to get to know you. I don't want anything to do with you."

"You don't want another hot fuck?" he whispered in my ear. "Next time, it could be somewhere crazy, like the train."

"The train?" I paused and looked up at him, willing my heart to stop beating so fast. "You want to fuck on the train?"

"Why not?" He shrugged, but I could see the huge grin on his face that he couldn't hide. "Shit, I'm not going to beg you to date me if all you want to do is fuck. I'm down for whatever."

Note to self and note to you—if a guy says that he is down for whatever, it means that he likes you. It means that he will try and be with you any way he can. It means that he wants to try and worm his way into your heart. I didn't know that then. I wish I had known that then.

"Fine. We'll fuck on the train. Wednesday." My words were short.

"Can I get your number?"

"No."

"How can we coordinate it?"

"Give me yours." I handed him my phone and waited for him to input it. "I'll text you on Wednesday an hour before I catch the train telling you which train and what time. You can't make it or you don't make it, then that's it."

"I do work, you know." He smiled at me. "I have business meetings I—"

"I don't give a fuck." I smiled at him sweetly. "We do this, we do it by my rules."

"Okay. So Wednesday, I'll be on high alert."

"Good for you."

"Maybe you'll let me buy you lunch or dinner or whatever after."

"I wouldn't count on it."

"You're a hard girl to get to know." He shook his head at me as we stood on the corner.

"I have a boyfriend." I wasn't sure why I told him. Maybe because I wanted to make him feel bad. Or maybe because I didn't want him to pursue me anymore. Maybe I wanted him to think I was a slut so he wouldn't keep giving me those smiles.

"I guess he's not doing something right." He laughed, though I could see from the look in his eyes that he was taken aback.

"Actually, he fucks me like he was made to do it." I grinned at him and ran my fingers down his chest. "I think I orgasm every single time from his cock alone."

He stared back at me then, and I could see that he was angry or offended or whatever handsome guys get when you subtly put them down.

"I don't know what happened to you, Saskia. Why you have up this wall, but I'm determined to figure you out. I'm determined to show you that all men aren't scum."

"Whatever." I rolled my eyes.

"My parents have a great marriage. They've been together for over thirty years now and they are still very much in love."

"Well bully for them." I leaned over and kissed him softly. "But now I have to go. Wait for my call."

And then I walked away. I could feel him watching me keenly. I walked quickly, my heart racing. I was scared. He had reacted in a way I hadn't expected.

I reached my apartment building and opened the door quickly and called Tom.

"Hey. What you doing?" I asked sweetly as soon as he picked up.

"I was about to take that girl, Alice, out on a lunch date. You remember her from the party a few nights ago?"

"Oh yeah. The cute girl with the short, blond hair?"

"Yeah. We've been seeing each other for a few weeks now. I think it could go somewhere—"

"I need you to cancel," I interrupted him. "I need you to come over."

"Now?"

"Yeah."

"Okay." He hung up, and I sat back on the couch.

I wish I could tell you that I felt bad for Alice. She had no idea that the guy she was seeing was about to ditch her so he could come and fuck me. She had no idea that I had him wrapped around my little finger. She'd seemed like a nice enough girl, but that wasn't my problem. What Tom did in his personal life was his business. I just knew that when I needed someone to fuck and hold me, Tom was the one to call.

He always made everything feel all right. Or rather, he made me forget my own problems. He was good for me that way. Or maybe he was just really bad for me. I don't know. And I really didn't care. I liked things to be numb. Numb was safe. Numb didn't make you feel like you wanted to die.

Tom arrived quickly. He always did. I suppose I was his drug as much as he was mine. I don't even think he told Alice he was ditching her because his phone rang and rang and rang as we fucked on the living room floor. I glanced at it, saw her name, and closed my eyes as I gripped the rug. That had been a mistake.

As soon as I closed my eyes, I saw Dominic's face. I imagined that it was him sliding in and out of me, holding on to my hips tightly. I quickly opened my eyes to forget his image, but I couldn't. He had already worked his way into my psyche.

I screamed as I orgasmed, my body enjoying the release, but mentally, all I could think about was Wednesday. Wednesday would be exciting and fun.

Wednesday, I'd get to fuck Dominic again. Wednesday, I'd get to stop the numbness and feel alive.

I froze as I realized that, for the first time in my life, I was actually looking forward to seeing a man.

I should have known then that something was going to go wrong. I should have known that Dominic, with all of his bravado and concern, wouldn't be able to accept everything. I should have known that no one is immune from love.

If only I'd decided to not text him that Wednesday. If I hadn't texted him, maybe everything in my life would still be okay. Unfortunately, I messed up and I did text. In fact, I texted before Wednesday. Those texts marked the beginning of the end for me. And it all started with a simple, "What you doing?"

CHAPTER FOUR

Sometimes I wonder what's wrong with me. I mean, I have to have some sort of psychological problems, right? Unless I'm a sociopath. Though I don't like blood and the thought of harming someone physically makes me feel sick. So I suppose that means I can't be a sociopath, right? No need to answer that. I doubt you know what my problem is, either.

I texted Dominic on Monday all day. I hadn't meant to. It just sort of happened. I told myself that it was nothing and that I was bored. It's boring being a kept woman. There are only so many shoes you can buy. Trust me, I know.

I was also feeling nervous—something I didn't usually feel. Aiden had stepped things up a bit. He wanted me to travel with him the next weekend. He said that I was going to be his assistant. Well, that was the official story. I didn't like it. I didn't want to have to go anywhere and have to lie, but it wasn't up to me.

He was going to pick me up Friday night and we were going to some work event or something. I didn't care that he wasn't going to introduce me as his girlfriend. I knew why he couldn't. I knew why and it didn't matter to me. I guess I'm a cold-hearted bitch like that. Well, I'm starting to think that I'm not so cold-hearted.

Meeting Dominic changed something in me. What can I say about Dominic that doesn't sound cliché or puke worthy? I guess I could tell you that he made me laugh. He makes me laugh good, old-fashioned, rip-roaring laughs that make my sides ache and my throat sore. He has a way with words. A way that's self-deprecating and amusing at the same time. He's complimentary, but he doesn't try too hard. It feels natural with him. As natural as anything can feel to me.

And he loves sex. And he's not ashamed to admit it. I'd never sexted with anyone before. I know you're shocked. How can I, queen of liberal sex, not have sexted? Well, I hadn't. Though now that I know what I was missing, that might change.

The First Time I Sexted

Dominic: What you up to?

Me: What do you care?

Dominic: I've been thinking about you.

Me: Oh?

Dominic: The bathroom scene keeps replaying in my mind.

Me: What bathroom scene?

Dominic: The one where I fucked you in Starbucks.

Me: I forgot, sorry.

Dominic: You won't forget me on the train.

Me: The train?

Dominic: You'll see.

Me: Will I?

Dominic: I hope so.

Me: Don't bet on it.

Five minutes passed and I wondered if he was upset.

Me: You alive?

Dominic: Why?

Me: Just checking.

Dominic: Thinking about me?

Me: Nope, sorry.

Dominic: I'm thinking about you.

Me: Ok.

Dominic: Wanna see?

Me: See what?

Dominic: This {attached image of the head on his cock}

Me: You just been in the shower?

Dominic: Why?

Dominic: Haha, funny.

Me: I'm glad you got that before I had to explain.

Dominic: You weren't complaining about the size when I fucked you.

Me: You're crude.

Dominic: I'm always crude when I masturbate.

Me: What?

Dominic: Send me a photo.

Me: Photo of what?

Dominic: Your breasts?

Dominic: Your pussy.

Dominic: Your fingers on your pussy.

Dominic: A dildo in your pussy.

Me: I get it.

Dominic: I'm waiting.

Ten minutes passed and I stared at the phone, wondering if I'd submit to his demand.

Dominic: Did I make you mad?

Dominic: Are you still going to let me fuck you on the train?

Me: You're obsessed with sex.

Dominic: I don't think you want to hear me talk about wanting to take you out to dinner.

Me: I'm not good enough for dinner?

Dominic: You're plenty good enough for dinner.

Me: Perv.

Dominic: Send me a photo of your fingers pinching your nipples.

Me: You wish.

Dominic: Come over.

Me: You're too handsome to be this desperate.

Dominic: You're too pretty to be a slut.

I have to admit that my heart stopped for a second then and I looked at the phone in anger. I felt hard and cold. I lay there for a second, confused at myself. I'd never been upset at being called a slut before. The word meant nothing to me. Words like that meant nothing. I knew who I was. And no one could tell me anything different.

Dominic: I'm sorry.

Dominic: Talk to me.

Dominic: Please.

Dominic: Fine, I'll whack off without your help.

Me: You're a jerk.

Dominic: You wouldn't talk to me if I wasn't.

Me: I have a boyfriend.

Dominic: You don't love him.

Me: I don't believe in love.

Dominic: You haven't dated me as yet :)

Me: Fine {attached photo of my breasts}

Dominic: I just came thinking about sucking your nipples.

Me: Sure.

Dominic: See {attached photo of his cock with cum covering the tip}

Me: Nice.

Dominic: You're turned on, aren't you?

Me: No.

Dominic: Touch yourself.

Me: No.

Dominic: Close your eyes and imagine my fingers are there.

Me: No.

Dominic: How does it feel?

Dominic: Stuck in the moment?

Dominic: Wishing it was me playing with you instead?

Dominic: If I was there, I'd have you on all fours and I'd be fucking you from behind.

Dominic: Did you fall asleep?

An hour later.

Dominic: Where did you go?

Me: Sorry, my boyfriend just came over and fucked me. I don't need to masturbate over the phone.

Dominic: You totally just played with yourself thinking of me, didn't you?

Dominic: Are you going back for round two?

Dominic: I am! :)

Me: I'll see you on the train.

Dominic: Don't wear any panties.

Me: I won't.

Dominic: So tell me, did you really just fuck or where you thinking of me?

Me: You'll never know.

I turned off my phone without waiting for a response from him and closed my eyes. I slipped my fingers back into my panties and imagined Dominic on top of me. I moaned softly as I thought about the photo he'd sent me with his large cock. I could imagine it slowly sliding in and out of me. I groaned as I felt my body tensing up again.

I froze as I realized what I was doing. I was fantasizing about a guy. I never did that. Fantasies were never about men I knew. They could never be about men I knew. It was okay to have sex with them. That was real. That was physical. That was instinctive. Fantasies got you in trouble.

I got off of my bed, ran into the bathroom, and took a shower. I didn't want to think of Dominic. He was absolutely nothing to me. Absolutely nothing.

I suppose now is the time that you're wondering, 'Why is Saskia so messed up?' Right? You're wondering, but you don't really want to know. No one does—not really. You don't want to know that my father is my uncle! Do you? How fucked up is that, right? My mom slept with her sister's husband after their wedding day. Though I can't say I blamed her. He had been her high school boyfriend. He'd cheated on my mom with her sister. She'd dumped his ass when she'd found out. He then married her sister and then he and my mom started sleeping with each other again. Then she got pregnant.

Everyone found out what had happened. You'd think my dad would be the one who was ostracized, right? Let's just say that my mom and I found ourselves in Section 8 and on food stamps with no one in the family talking to either of us. Not that I knew or cared. I was a baby.

I hate telling my story. Every girl who fucks around has daddy issues. I hate it. I don't want to be that statistic. I don't want to be the girl who can't love because her father is her uncle and her mom sleeps all day and smokes weed all night. Who wants to be that statistic? And to be fair, I'm not that girl. I'm not fucked up because of my parents, though I should be. I'm fucked up for another reason entirely. But I don't want to talk about that. Not now.

I suppose you're wondering how I can just sleep around. All these different men, Saskia. Are you judging me? Are you, bitch? I don't take well to people judging me. Who the fuck cares who I sleep with? So I have a boyfriend, a friend with benefits, a new hook-up, and random sex with strangers. What's it to you?

I know I'm being dumb. Trust me. I worry about getting pregnant all the time. And I worry about STDs. I do.

I know what you're thinking. How worried can I be if I still have random sex? I ask myself that every time I have a scare. I go to the free clinic every month, though. And I buy condoms. I just don't always remember to use them.

I know. You can judge me now. I'm dumb as fuck. I'm irresponsible. I'm a health hazard to myself and others. But some days, I just don't care.

Well, now I do. What made me change? Dominic, of course. It had to be Dominic. Life's funny like that. It always brings you that one person who changes everything. People call that person the game changer. That's the man or woman who changes everything you think about love and life. That's the person who makes you want to be a better person. I suppose it had to happen, right? That's the beauty of life. We all meet that person. And well, for someone like me, it had to be Dominic. It could only have been Dominic. That's karma for you!

***

Wednesday came and I was excited. It made me nervous being so excited. I mean, I never got excited. Excited means that you care and I don't care. I never cared. But when Dominic's text came, I almost squealed.

Dominic: Catch the 1 train at 5pm from 50th. I'm going to get on at 116th Street. Get into the second cabin. Don't look for me. I'll find you.

Me: Don't look for you?

Dominic: You'll feel me before you see me.

Me: I see.

Dominic: Don't forget, no panties.

Me: Only if you wear no pants.

Dominic: You wish.

Me: It's only fair.

Dominic: I'm excited to see you.

Me: How excited?

Dominic: I'm harder than stale bread.

I burst out laughing then. No one had ever made me laugh so much before.

Dominic: I hope I didn't scare you off.

Me: Think before you text.

Dominic: Are we crazy?

Me: What do you think?

Dominic: I think I'm crazy about you.

Me: You don't know me.

Dominic: Do I need to?

Me: I'll see you on the train.

Dominic: The hand you feel on your ass will be mine.

Me: It better be. I hate taking trains.

Dominic: Aww, slumming for me?

Me: Slumming with you, yes.

Dominic: I wish I could spend this weekend with you.

Me: I'm going out of town.

Dominic: So am I.

Me: Good for you.

Dominic: My parents wouldn't approve of you.

Me: And I care because?

Dominic: I don't care either.

Me: Uh huh.

Dominic: I'd give up my inheritance for you.

Me: All $10.

Dominic: All $100 Million, yes.

Holy shit! His family was worth a $100 million?

Dominic: Don't tell me I scared you off because I'm rich.

Me: You can't scare a gold-digger off.

Dominic: You're not a gold-digger, and even if you were, I wouldn't care.

I turned off my phone then and put it in my handbag. His comments were making me think things I really didn't want to think. This was about sex. Not cutesy comments and loaded reassurances. It was all about sex, sex, sex. I needed to remind myself of that fact.

***

"Come here often?" he whispered in my ear as his hand massaged my ass through my skirt.

I didn't answer him and I didn't look at him. I could see an old man staring at us, and I just smiled to myself.

"Oh, so we're playing it as strangers?" he whispered, and I felt his tongue inside my ear.

Once again, I didn't move, and I could tell that excited him because his breathing was heavy. His hands continued to squeeze my butt, and I pretended that I didn't feel it.

We stood like that for a few minutes before the train stopped in the tunnel and everything went black.

Some people started complaining, but I found myself grinning as his fingers eagerly lifted up my skirt. His pushed his hands between my legs and started gently rubbing me.

"You're so wet," he groaned as he stuck two fingers inside me, and I could feel my body trembling at his touch. "You're a dirty girl, aren't you?" He withdrew his fingers and pulled me back towards him.

I felt his hardness pushed up against my ass, and I reached behind and grabbed him. He groaned out loud, and suddenly, it went quiet in the carriage.

"Did you hear that?" one lady spoke in the darkness.

"I think someone is fucking," a man said crudely.

Dominic's fingers crept up under my shirt and started playing with my nipples. I rubbed my ass back into him and felt him undoing his zipper and taking his manhood out.

"Bend over," he spoke loudly, and I flushed in the dark. Now everyone knew that two people were definitely having sex.

"What did you say, Gerry?" an older-sounding lady asked.

"I didn't say anything."

"Back that ass up," Dominic said loudly, and I heard someone gasp.

I shivered as I realized what we were doing, but I bent over and backed my ass into him.

"Good girl." He pulled my hips towards him and I felt his cock enter me with such force that I fell forward slightly.

"Ooh!" I cried out, not bothering to be quiet.

"Omg, someone is definitely fucking," the man said again.

Dominic paused then and started moving slowly. His cock moved in and out of me, teasing every inch of me, and I could feel myself getting wetter and wetter.

"Go faster!" I gasped.

"What?" I could hear the grin in his voice.

"Go faster!" I shouted, and I heard a collective gasp. I didn't care though because his cock was slamming into me so hard that I couldn't even think properly. "I'm going to come!" I screamed and moaned as I felt him coming inside of me as I orgasmed.

The train started moving then, and I felt him withdraw from me. I stood up, pulled my skirt down, and held on to the bar. The lights flickered back on and I could see a look of shock on everyone's face as they looked around the carriage, trying to figure out who'd been fucking.

I looked behind me to see if I saw Dominic, but he was no longer there. I was curious as to where he'd gone, but I didn't want to be obvious. I knew I was going to get off at the next stop and take a taxi home.

"I hope you had a good fuck," the old man whispered to me as we got off of the train.

"I don't know what you're talking about." I gave him a puzzled look, and he laughed.

"I'd believe you if I wasn't staring at your nipple right now." His eyes glazed over, and I felt his fingers on me before I could stop him. "If you want seconds, let me know." He squeezed my right nipple and I froze in shock.

"Get your hands off of her."

Out of nowhere, I saw Dominic hitting the man and glaring at him in anger. The man stumbled and looked shocked that he'd been hit. Dominic grabbed my arm and pulled me with him out of the station.

"Are you okay?" He looked at me with concerned eyes, and I nodded. "I could kill that man."

"It's okay." I touched his arm and saw that he was still angry. "Trust me, it's okay."

"When I saw him touch you…" He frowned and shook his head.

I stared at him for a moment, wondering what I should do. I was touched by his concern, but I was also worried. I didn't want him to fall for me. I didn't want to fall for him.

"Spend the night with me." He looked into my eyes and ran his hands through his hair. "I know you want to say no, but please, just say yes."

"I can't." I shook my head.

"Yes, you can." He grabbed my hands. "I promise no talking. Just fucking."

"Okay. Just fucking," I agreed reluctantly.

I knew I was playing with fire. I knew I shouldn't go back to his place. Nothing good could come from us liking each other.

"I'll even let you give me head." He grinned, and I laughed.

"Whatever."

"Shall we go?" He looked calmer now, and I realized that it felt easy with him. Everything about him made me feel calm and relaxed, and it scared me.

"No." I shook my head. "Let's go to a club I know."

"A club?" He frowned.

"It's a swingers club." I stared at him defiantly. He had to know that this wasn't going to be anything special.

"Fine." He nodded slowly. "Let's go."

"Oh." I frowned. "You want to fuck someone else?" I was angry that he'd agreed so easily.

"Don't you?" He raised an eyebrow.

"Let's just go to your place." I walked to the road and flagged down a cab. "But just fucking, no talking."

"Fine." He grinned at me as we got in. "Sixty percent fucking and forty percent talking."

"Fine." I rolled my eyes. "But that's only because I have to tell you what to do."

"Uh huh." His fingers slipped between my legs and started rubbing my clit. I saw the cab driver's eyes pop open as he saw what was going on in his back seat. "You can tell me how to make you wet when we get to my place." He laughed as his fingers easily slid back and forth in my wetness. "I'll be grateful for the advice."

I closed my eyes and groaned. If I'd known how everything was going to go down, I would have jumped out of that cab then and there. If I'd known what was going to happen, I never would have gone home with Dominic that night.

CHAPTER FIVE

Do you believe in foreshadowing? I never used to. I mean, how can events occurring now predict what's going to happen in my future? It's not like this is *The Twilight Zone* or anything. Though I'm starting to wonder if I was wrong before. Maybe that feeling you feel in your bones is real.

Being with Dominic made me feel alive and happy. That's something I'd never really felt before and it scared me. I knew it couldn't last. Happiness never lasts for people like me.

I know, I know. I need to get a grip. I'm hot. I'm sexy. I'm not wanting for money. I have men chasing me. That stuff doesn't make you happy. You know that. I know that. Happiness is a state of mind and all that crap. It truly is.

When I was with Dominic, I felt like a part of me was flying. I was soaring through the air on a jet stream and the world was passing me by in multicolor fusion. I'd never felt that way before. I hadn't expected to ever feel this way. It was just so easy. Too easy.

I knew I was in trouble when I realized I wanted to blow off my weekend with Aiden to be with Dominic. I never blow off my weekends with Aiden. It all started with a simple text.

Dominic: Come away with me this weekend.

Me: To your parents' place?

Dominic: Don't be crazy.

Me: Oh, you don't like taking your hos home?

Dominic: Do you really want to meet my parents?

Me: No :)

Dominic: I'll blow off my parents and you blow off whatever you're doing.

Me: You mean who I'm doing?

Dominic: I don't want to think about it.

Me: I can't.

Dominic: You can.

Me: I don't want to.

Dominic: Liar.

And he was right, of course. I did want to blow off Aiden. I wasn't looking forward to the weekend. Normally, I got off on sneaking around and having his colleagues wonder who I was. I was just that bit too sexy to be a real assistant, but they never questioned him, of course. No one questions the man with the money.

Dominic: You know you'll be thinking of me when you're with him.

Me: Do you really want to discuss this?

Dominic: What do you think?

Me: Then drop it.

Dominic: Drop him and come away with me this weekend.

Me: You're crazy. What about your parents?

Dominic: I can see them anytime. I'd rather be fucking you.

Me: So romantic.

Dominic: You don't want romance.

Me: You could pretend I do.

Dominic: Why pretend?

Me: This is all about sex for you, isn't it?

Dominic: What do you think?

I knew it wasn't. I knew he liked me. I knew he wanted me to be more than just his friend with benefits. I knew that, and a part of me wanted it as well. A very small part. I mean, I'm not the sort of girl who does commitment. It wasn't in my DNA.

Dominic: Fine, don't drop your weekend plans. Can I call?

Me: Why?

Dominic: I'd rather have phone sex than text sex.

Me: I'd rather have real sex.

Dominic: I can be over in 30 minutes.

Me: Just call me.

Dominic: Scaredy-cat.

Me: I don't know if Aiden is coming over tonight or in the am.

Dominic: I can't believe he doesn't know you're fucking other guys

Me: He doesn't like to share.

Dominic: I don't want to hear about him. :(

Me: You brought it up.

Dominic: I don't like to share either.

Me: Call me.

The phone rang ten seconds later, and I waited for it to ring five times before I answered.

"Why do you love playing with me, Saskia?" His breathing was heavy, and I knew he was already turned on.

"Why do you love me playing with you, Dominic?"

"I hate that you have a boyfriend," he muttered. "I want you to be mine. All mine."

"Well, we all want things we can't have."

"What does he have that I don't?"

"A big cock."

"Bitch." He laughed, and I joined him.

"He doesn't call me mean names, either."

"I bet if he knew you were hooking up with me, he would."

"Perhaps." I closed my eyes and smiled. "If he knew about any of you other guys, he'd be pissed."

"There are others?" I could hear a tinge of jealousy in his voice.

"No," I lied. He didn't need to know about Tom. No one needed to know about him.

"There are others, aren't there?"

"No," I lied again, not wanting him to know the truth.

"So it's just me and Aiden."

"Yes."

"So it's soon-to-be just me?"

"Dominic," I whispered, wanting to change the subject.

"I can take care of you as well."

"I don't want that." I shook my head even though he couldn't see me.

"Why not?" He sounded annoyed.

"Just because." I sighed. I didn't want him to take care of me because then things would change. I'd be the girl who owed him. He'd have expectations. I'd lose my power. I'd lose everything I now had with him.

"Whatever." His voice was exasperated. "I'm sure I have more money than him."

"It's not about money."

"I can fuck you every which way you like."

"I'm not going to talk about this."

"Are your panties on?"

"Yes."

"Take them off. Now," he commanded me, and I grinned into the phone. "Are they still on?" he asked again about a minute later.

"Yes," I whispered as I pulled them off.

"Don't make me come over there," he growled. "Are they off now?"

"Yes, master."

"Say it again like you mean it."

"Yes, master."

"Close your eyes," he muttered. "Close your eyes and put your fingers between your legs. Does it feel good?"

"Yes," I moaned, and he laughed.

"I bet you're so wet right now," he groaned. "Shit, I want to taste you so badly right now. I wish I was there."

"That would have been nice." I whimpered into the phone as I played with myself. I writhed on the bed and froze when I heard footsteps. "Gotta go." I hung up the phone quickly and looked up in surprise as Aiden walked in.

"Hey." He walked over to me and gave me a kiss on the cheek.

"Hey." I sat up and nodded.

"I figured I should come over tonight. Prepare you for the weekend."

"It's fine." I rolled my eyes. "All your workmates will think I'm your assistant."

"You're not coming away for a work weekend." He shook his head and grinned at me. "You're coming home with me."

"Oh." My eyes widened. "Are you sure that's a good idea?"

"Yes." His mouth found mine and his tongue licked my lips as his fingers found their way to my pussy. "Hmmm, been playing with yourself?" He grinned as he rubbed my clit and found my wetness.

"I was horny."

"I guess I came over right on time." He grunted and pushed two fingers inside me.

"Oh." I groaned and closed my eyes. His fingers were rough as he fingered me, and an image of Dominic popped into my mind.

"You have to be smart this weekend." He withdrew his fingers and sucked on them as he pulled away from me. "I want to have some fun, but we cannot get caught."

"But won't your wife—" I started and frowned.

"That's the beauty of it." He grinned. "That makes it more fun."

"I don't know." I shook my head.

It wasn't like I didn't know he was married. Yes, I'm that kind of bitch. I knew and I didn't care. It wasn't my problem. That's how I felt, but I'd never been around the wife. I'd been the other woman at work events, but never around the actual wife.

"It's not up to you." He grabbed me around the waist and flipped me over. "I like to play with fire."

"What if she figures something out?" I whispered against the sheet as he pulled me up onto my knees. I heard him undoing his zipper and felt the tip of his cock against me.

"She won't." He groaned and entered me from behind. "Shit, I've been waiting all day for this." He grabbed my hips and slammed into me hard, his cock seeming to go deeper and deeper with each entry.

I felt his hands grabbing my breasts, and I closed my eyes as he brought me to the edge of an orgasm. I screamed as he moved faster and faster. I could feel my body trembling, and it quaked as we both came together pretty quickly. I fell down onto the bed and he rolled down next to me.

"We just have to play it cool."

"I don't know why you want me to come." I looked over at him and touched his face, looking into his eyes with concern. "Is everything okay?"

"Things have never been better." His green eyes crinkled as he stared at me. "I don't know why you're questioning me."

"Just seems pretty risky." I shrugged.

"Since when have you cared?"

"I don't." I smiled at him and ran my finger down his chest. "I don't care at all."

"Good. My son and his girlfriend will be there. I'm sure my wife will be occupied with them."

"Don't you think they'll be wondering why I'm there?"

"I always bring work home."

"Other assistants?"

"Yes."

"I see."

"You want to know if I fuck them as well?" He laughed as he looked at me, and I shook my head.

"Actually, no."

"Good, that's why I like you, Saskia. You're not all up in my business."

"Yeah."

"And of course, I like that your pussy is mine. Any time I want it." He laughed. "And it's worth every penny I pay. Ten thousand a month for grade-A pussy is hard to beat."

"You make me sound like a prostitute." I frowned.

"You never cared before." He shrugged and closed his eyes. "Plus, you get to call yourself my girlfriend."

I rolled over then, suddenly not feeling so sure about any of the decisions I had made. Was I really proud of calling myself the girlfriend of a married man who had no respect for me? All I could think about was Dominic as I lay there, and I grew angry at myself.

Dominic was making me wish for things I had no right to wish for. I'd always been satisfied with the arrangement Aiden and I had. It was fine. It was perfect. I didn't care that he was married. I really didn't care. I tried to ignore the small itch of worry that was settling in my stomach and telling me that I was a bad person.

I wasn't bad—I was just a realist. I looked out for myself first and foremost. I couldn't stop myself from thinking that. Not because some cute guy made me think that perhaps there was more to life than fucking. I wasn't going to let Dominic make me start to believe in love.

The Awkward Moment I Met the Wife

If you're human and you have any sort of emotion or heart, you will feel bad meeting your lover's wife. I know that now. It's one thing to be the mistress and ignore the fact that he's married, but when you meet the wife, it's a whole other ballgame. I know you think that I'm an evil bitch. What sort of woman sleeps with a married man, knowing that he's married? Call me a ho, a slut, a home wrecker—whatever you want. It's likely true.

I didn't think I was going to care when I met his wife. I thought the act would be quite simple. It wasn't. She was nice. Really sweet. Really friendly and welcoming, and she had no idea. I'd expected her to be a frigid bitch. Or something. However, she was anything but that. I felt bad instantly. And then I felt angry at myself for feeling bad.

"You're Mr. X's new assistant?" she asked me formally. I nodded, and she smiled. "I love meeting his assistants."

I wanted to ask her how many she'd met and how she could be so dumb, but I kept my mouth shut.

"I hope you like the room." She showed me to a huge bedroom. "My son and his girlfriend will be next door. They arrive tomorrow."

"Oh, okay." I nodded again.

"Please feel free to make yourself at home." She gave me a big smile. "I'm sure Mr. X will let you know where the office is. Don't let him work you too hard."

"I'll try not to." I nodded and smiled back at her, though my smile was very, very weak.

I watched as she walked out of the door and tried not to feel bad. It wasn't my problem. I suppose you want to know why I'm calling him Mr. X? Well, he's someone you would likely know and his real name isn't Aiden. I figured, if it turns out that you have a big mouth, all of my bases are covered.

KNOCK KNOCK

"Come in!" I called out, trying to pretend I was happy.

"I'm going to need you in the office in ten minutes for some work." Aiden smiled at me.

"Yes, sir."

"Do you know where the office is?"

"No."

"Go to the kitchen and then walk down the corridor. It will be two doors on the left."

"Okay." I nodded.

"Are you wearing panties?"

"Yes."

"That's fine." He shrugged. "I only want a blowjob."

"Okay." I stared at him, and he grinned.

"This is going to be such a good weekend." He laughed and walked out of the door.

I sat on the bed for a few minutes and felt quite sorry for myself.

"*Have fun with your parents*," I texted Dominic and laughed when he responded immediately.

"*Thanks. They are killing me. My dad and I are playing golf right now and I want to die.*"

"*Sounds fun.*"

"*I'd rather be with you.*"

I looked at the text, smiled, and texted back quickly before I could stop myself.

"*I'd rather be with you too.*"

"*OMG*," he texted back. "*Did I just read that right?*"

"*Don't get a big head?*"

"*I can't lie, my dick is hard now. :)*"

"Have fun with that."

"Can I see you on Monday?"

"Maybe."

"Drop Aiden. I'll take care of you."

"I can't have you doing that."

"Be my girlfriend."

"No."

"Please?"

"Maybe," I typed back and laughed. I couldn't believe I had said that.

"Yes! ;)"

"I have to go."

"Until Monday."

I pushed my phone back in my pocket, walked to the bathroom, and sat on the bathtub. I decided that I wasn't going to go to the office to suck Aiden off. I was taking a stand. I wasn't going to let him do that to me. I was finally over it. I didn't want to be the other woman. I wanted to give Dominic a chance. Everything about him seemed to gel with me. I wanted to see what could happen between us.

***

Mrs. X knocked on my door and then walked in. "Hello, dear. Just wanted to let you know dinner is ready."

"Thank you." I smiled and followed her out of the room.

"There you are." Mr. X looked up at me and frowned.

"Sorry. I fell asleep." I shrugged. "Hopefully I can catch up on the work you wanted after dinner."

"I suppose so." His eyes glinted into mine. "There's a lot I need you to do."

"That's fine." I nodded, and we all sat down at the table.

"Jessie called. She and Evan will be home late tonight."

"I thought they were coming tomorrow?"

"She said Evan got done with his meeting early."

"Okay."

"I think he's going to propose soon."

"It's about time." Aiden nodded. "They need to settle down."

"I know Jessie's ready." She smiled at me. "Jessie and Evan have been dating for three years now. I know she's anxious for him to propose."

"Evan is your son?" I smiled politely.

"Yes." She smiled again. "He's been a bit of a playboy. I'll be happy to see him married."

"Don't rush the boy," Aiden muttered. "He'll back out if you say anything."

"We're both anxious for him to marry Jessie." She laughed. "We both think she's perfect for him."

"She's a good girl." Aiden nodded and smiled at me. I looked at him curiously, wondering how good this Jessie really was.

Dinner was a pretty quick affair. Mrs. X wasn't super hungry, and Aiden hurried to his office as soon as he was done.

"I'll come for you when I'm ready." He nodded at me, and I just nodded back and walked to my room.

I sat on my bed and wondered how I was going to tell Aiden that it was over. The hours seemed to go by slowly, and it must have been about ninc p.m. when I heard a knock on the door.

"Come in." I jumped up, and he walked in with a grin.

"I need to fuck you now." He walked over to the bed and pulled his tie off.

"I need to talk to you, Aiden." I took a step back and fell onto the bed.

"We can talk afterwards."

"What if your wife walks in?"

"She won't." He grinned. "She's gone to bed."

"Oh." I looked up at him and felt his fingers on my breasts.

"Take your clothes off," he commanded, grunting.

"I'm tired." I shook my head, and he paused, looking down at me with surprise in his eyes.

"Oh?" His fingers ran up the inside of my thighs and pulled my panties to the side. "I think you've got some energy left in you."

"I don't know." I closed my eyes and widened my legs automatically as he played with me.

He laughed as he rubbed me gently and then pulled my panties and skirt off. "I think you're okay," he said, pulling me up. He pulled my top off and then undid my bra. I watched as he pulled his pants and shirt off.

"Are you sure this is smart?" I looked up at him in wonder.

"I want you to ride me." He got onto the bed and pulled me on top of him.

I looked down at him and closed my eyes. I guessed that it didn't matter if I fucked him one last time. I gently started moving back and forth on him. His hands reached up and grabbed my breasts. He pinched my nipples hard, and I moaned. It felt dangerous and sexy being with him.

The tip of his cock teased me for a few minutes before he grabbed my hips and pulled me down on top of him. I moved up and down on him quickly, enjoying the feel of him inside me. I'd miss fucking him. He was always hard. He always went deep, and I always came.

I groaned as he grabbed my hips and moved me faster and faster on top of him. I found myself enjoying the deep thrusts of him inside me, and I was just about to come when I heard the door opening.

"Oh, sorry," a young female voice said, sounding shocked.

I looked behind me and froze as I stared back at the door.

"Jessie, close the fucking door!" Aiden looked up at her and shouted at her with such force, but she continued to stare at both of us with wide eyes.

I stared back at her, wondering what to do, but it seemed like Aiden had no such worries as he grabbed ahold of my hips and started moving me back and forth on him.

"What's going on, Jessie?" A man's voice joined Jessie at the door, but I didn't turn around this time. If Aiden didn't care, I sure didn't, and I was so close to orgasm that I didn't want to move.

"Evan, take Jessie and get out of the room." Aiden's voice was angry, and I looked around quickly to see if his son looked shocked to see his father fucking another girl.

That's when my heart sank. Everything seemed to go in slow motion then.

Aiden lifted me off of him and placed me on all fours. I felt his cock quickly slide into me, and he laughed when his fingers reached around to grab my breasts as I came against him. I closed my eyes and allowed my body to enjoy the orgasm that was exploding in my body.

"Evan, get out of here," Aiden muttered again as he exploded inside of me.

Evan stared at us both with blank eyes as we orgasmed on the bed and then slowly closed the door. I kept my mind blank and tried not to allow the pain I was feeling to seep into my bones.

"What is it you wanted to talk about?" Aiden fondled my breasts as we lay back in the bed, breathing heavily.

"Nothing." I closed my eyes and took a few deep breaths.

It didn't matter now. Not now that I knew that Aiden's son Evan was actually Dominic. My Dominic had looked as shocked as I had felt. We had both been caught and I knew in my heart that there was no turning back from this moment.

CHAPTER SIX

I suppose you think I should have left the house right then and there. Any normal person would have, but I'm not normal. A part of me was still in shock. I couldn't believe that he'd seen me with his dad, and I also couldn't believe that he had a girlfriend, almost fiancée. It didn't seem real.

How could he have a girlfriend if he'd been texting me all week long? I thought he really liked me. I always prided myself on being smarter than the average woman. No disrespect to any suckers out there, but the lies men tell usually don't work on me. I know a bullshitter from a bullshitter. I'm not that average girl who sits in her room crying because her guy doesn't call her or seems to be acting cold. I'm not that girl because I don't care what the fuck a guy has to say.

I don't cry and I don't complain. And I never get my heart broken.

Pain is for those pitiful women who don't know how to live without a man. I know I'm a hypocrite. But there's one key distinction between me and most women—all I want is sex. Well, I guess I should say that there *was* one key distinction if the pain in my heart was anything to go by.

I'm part of the ranks now. I'm pitiful.

I was grateful that Aiden left the bedroom pretty soon after Dominic. He didn't even know that we had a connection. Part of me was glad that he hadn't realized that his son and I had had a moment. If I'd been thinking clearly and not preoccupied with my own drama, I would have noticed that he and Jessie had had a moment.

It's at this point that most people get hopeful. They think, 'Ooh, Dominic will dump his cheating bitch of a girl, Jessie, and I'll dump Aiden and we'll live happily ever after.' I already told you that my life is no fairy tale. I'm here to tell you that sometimes dirty-dog deeds follow dirty dogs in all different ways.

At the end of the day, I haven't been the best kind of girl. But don't despair just yet. My story gets better and worse. Just not in the ways that you think.

I'll admit it now, though it's something I've never wanted to admit. I was falling in love with Dominic. I guess, at the end of the day, I'm like every other woman. I want love. We can all pretend and hide it. Numbness can hold a lot of things in, but ultimately we were all made for love. Love love love. Just thinking the word makes me feel sick.

I took a shower as soon as Aiden left the room. I scrubbed my body so hard. It was the first time I'd truly felt dirty during sex and that was due to the guilt. The guilt was due to his being married, though. All I could think of was his wife. His poor wife not knowing what was going on.

Yeah, I was mad about Dominic, and I was pissed that he'd seen me riding his dad, but he knew that I had a boyfriend. If anything, I had more right to be mad at him. His lies and sweet talk had been nothing but acting.

This is the point where you expect me to say that I dumped Aiden. I should have, right? I did feel guilty. I did feel ashamed. However, I also thought about my apartment and my bank account. I thought about my life and I knew that I'd just deal with the guilt. I told you I'm a cold-hearted bitch sometimes.

That's what Tom calls me. He doesn't care if he hurts me with his words. He doesn't, of course. I like it. Sometimes I have him talk dirty to me during sex. It turns me on more with him. He'd get a laugh out of the whole situation when I told him. I knew he'd been feeling out this last week as I hadn't called him to come over once.

As I walked out of the shower and into my bedroom, a wicked thought crossed my mind. I picked up my phone, texted Tom, and gave him Aiden's address. I was going to have him come up and stay the weekend.

I told you I was wicked. I thought it would be great fun to stir the pot up a little bit more, partly because I was angry and partly because I was jealous.

Of course, Tom texted me back immediately. He was going to show up first thing in the morning. It was perfect.

The moment I realized that I was just like every other sad girl

About ten minutes after I stepped out of the shower, there was a knock on my door. I didn't bother to get up and answer it. I didn't want to see Aiden again tonight. The knock came again. This time it was louder and more insistent.

"Can I come in?" Dominic's voice was loud and insistent as he opened the door and walked into the room.

"I didn't say yes." I didn't look up at him.

"So you're fucking my dad." He spoke the words softly and distastefully.

"Don't judge me." I looked up then and cringed at the look on his face.

"Did you know?"

"How was I supposed to know?" I stared into his eyes as he walked closer to me.

"I don't know." He shrugged.

"So what's your name? Dominic or Evan?"

"It's Dominic." He ran his hands through his hair. "I was christened Evan Dominic, but I prefer Dominic. My parents prefer Evan."

"Uh huh."

"You're fucking my dad."

"You've got a girlfriend," I spat out, trying to ignore the jealousy stirring in my stomach.

"Is that a problem?" He raised an eyebrow at me, and I wanted to slap him.

"Would have been nice if you'd told me."

"Is he a good lay?" He leaned towards me so that I could feel his breath on my lips. "Do you think of me when he fucks you or do you think of him when I fuck you? Or do you fantasize about us both fucking you at the same time?"

"You're sick." I slapped him hard across the face.

"I shouldn't be jealous, right?" He laughed bitterly. "I knew you had a boyfriend. I knew you were fucking someone else."

"Stop it." I pushed past him, and he grabbed me around the waist and pulled me back towards him. "Let go of me."

"I should have known you were a mistress," he whispered against my hair as his hands moved up and down my back. "I should have known that the man you were seeing had a wife."

"Don't do this," I said, groaning as his fingers worked their way up to my breasts. "Dominic," I moaned as he pinched my nipples.

"I don't know if I'm madder at you for doing this and ruining my family, or at my dad for cheating on my mom."

"You're cheating on your girlfriend with me." I closed my eyes and pushed my body against his. "You're no better than me," I muttered.

"Jessie's not the one." His lips pressed down on mine.

"And I am?" I whispered up at him, but he didn't answer. Instead, his tongue entered my mouth and his fingers fell to my ass.

"I want to make love to you." His words sounded urgent, and I couldn't say no.

Part of me jumped at his words. He'd said 'make love.' 'Make love' meant something completely different than fucking. Maybe he understood that what I had with his father didn't affect what we had together. His father meant nothing to me. Not when compared to him.

"Are you sure?" I pulled back and looked into his eyes.

"I need to feel you." His lips crushed down on mine again and he pushed me down onto the bed. "I want to hear you moan for me," he continued as his fingers roughly rubbed against me.

"That hurts." I pushed him away.

"Then hurt me too." His eyes flashed at me. "Hurt me, Saskia."

"I don't want to hurt you." I lay back as he stared down at me. His hands were pinning my arms down and I could barely move.

"I can't touch you." He fell down on the bed next to me. "I can't do it."

"You despise me now?" I whispered softly, more hurt than I'd ever been in my life.

"I don't despise you." He looked at me for a second. "Do I think you're a cheap bitch? Yes, but what can I say?"

"Your words don't hurt me," I lied. "You're not exactly a prince."

"You fucked my dad."

"I know. I was there," I retorted. "Stop reminding me."

"Do I mean so little to you?" His eyes narrowed. "How could you?"

"I'm not the one in the wrong here." I sat up and pulled his zipper down. "I'm not going to let you treat me like a leper." I quickly pulled his cock out.

He was already hard, and I quickly dropped down to take him in my mouth. He tasted salty and briny as I sucked on him long and hard. I heard him groan as I took him as deep as I could. I felt his hands on my head pushing me down, and I knew he was close to coming by the way his body went tense.

I quickly stopped sucking him and moved so that I was on top of him. I slipped my panties to the side and gently eased myself down on him. He stared up at me as I rode him slowly, enjoying the feel of him inside me. He grabbed my hips and rocked me back and forth on him. Neither of us spoke as I continued riding him. I increased my pace and bobbed up and down on him quickly. His cock felt like heaven as I moved and his fingers roughly played with me, bringing me closer to climax. I stopped for one brief second and he grabbed my hands as we both orgasmed at the same time.

"Fuck!" he shouted as he came inside me fast and furious.

"Oh, Dominic." I collapsed next to him and stroked his hair as we lay there panting.

He stared at me for a few seconds and sat up. "Thanks." He gave me a kiss on the cheek. "Oh, and I forgot to answer your question."

"What question?" I lay back and stared at him. I was still panting from the hot sex, and I could barely keep my eyes open.

"When you asked if you were the one." He jumped up and pulled up his zipper. "The answer's no, I don't think you are." His eyes looked at me with a hint of anger and he turned away from me in silence.

I watched him walk to the door with my face burning. I thought my heart was going to break in two, and I just lay there staring up at the ceiling. I tried not to think about anything, but I couldn't stop a solitary tear from rolling down my cheek. It was at that moment that I realized I was just as pitiful as every other girl.

***

There are two things you can do when you've been rejected. You can sit around and feel sorry for yourself. You can let your tears give you comfort. You can let the empty hole in your heart comfort you as you wallow in your nothingness. Or you get up and make them regret it. Because the secret is that you can make him regret it. Even if he's the one who dumped you and made you feel bad.

Men don't like feeling like they've given up something good. Or something that another man wants. It's the ego in them. Every man has an ego. Every man is human. You can always make them regret it. You just have to stop crying your eyes out before time runs out.

That's one good thing about me. I think with my head first. Well, I try to. I hadn't thought with my head when I'd slept with Dominic again. I'd known it was too soon, but part of me had wanted to believe that sex would bring us back to that spot. That spot that felt like home. I'd been wrong. All it had done was made him think of me sleeping with his dad.

I knew that was true because a part of me had been thinking about his dad while I had been riding him. I know that sounds crazy. Or maybe even sick, but I couldn't stop myself. It's not something I'm proud of, but it's also not something I'm going to be ashamed of. Neither one of them was better than me. Neither one of them was a saint. In fact, all three of us were in the wrong. Yet, somehow, I was the pariah. All because I'm the female in the situation. Well, fuck that.

I fell asleep pretty quickly after Dominic had left. I was too mentally exhausted to think about everything that had happened. And yeah, I felt like a slut. A tiny part of me felt like a big old rejected slut and there was nothing I could do to fix that.

***

Tom arrived at seven a.m. the next morning. I was grinning as I opened the front door to let him in even though I was still tired as hell.

"It's seven a.m.." I groaned as we walked to the bedroom.

"It sounded like you needed me urgently." He shrugged.

"How's your girlfriend?"

"It's over." He shrugged again and then frowned. "You okay?"

"I've been better."

"I can't believe you're here at Aiden's house." He sighed. "Is his wife here?"

"What do you think?"

"Are you kidding me?" His eyes widened as we walked into the bedroom I was sleeping in. "This place is nice."

"Yeah, it is." I grinned and walked over to the bed. "Now I'm going back to sleep."

"What?"

"I'm still tired." I snuggled into the pillow. "You can join me if you want."

"Is that a good idea?" His eyes lit up.

"No sex." I yawned. "I'm too tired."

"You're never too tired." He laughed.

"Tom."

"Fine." He flopped down on the bed next to me. "By the way, Natasha is worried about you."

"Why?" I snuggled into his chest. It was always comfortable being with Tom.

"Why do you think?" He played with my hair and then rubbed my shoulder. "She thinks that you're pretty close to a breakdown."

"What is she talking about?" I sighed and snuggled in closer to him. I felt his lips on my forehead, so soft and warm, and I smiled. "I'm so glad you're here, by the way."

"How glad?" He looked at me and smiled.

"This glad." I leaned up and kissed him.

His tongue easily slipped into my mouth, and we lay there kissing for a few minutes. I closed my eyes and pictured Dominic. This was how I wished it were with him. Though I guess part of the allure of being with him was that it wasn't so easy.

"So why exactly am I here?"

"You're here because I want to make him sweat." I grinned.

"I thought you didn't want Aiden to know about us?"

"I didn't, but everything's changed." I didn't tell him about Dominic. "It's not like he can say anything." I grinned. "His wife is here."

"I don't understand why you care about making him jealous."

"Do you care?" I sighed, annoyed at his continued questioning.

"I'm curious." His fingers cupped my breasts. "I want to know—"

"Shh." I placed a finger on his lips. "No more talking."

"What?" He laughed.

"I've got an itch." I raised an eyebrow, and he grinned.

"Well, let me scratch it." Tom knew exactly what I was talking about, and he eagerly crawled under the sheets and the duvet.

I quickly pulled my panties down, spread my legs, and lay back. I wasn't particularly in the mood for anything, but I didn't want him asking too many questions. I didn't want to have to talk about what had happened. Not yet. It still felt too raw and fresh. I still felt too cheap. And too used—something I had promised myself I would never let a man make me feel.

Tom's tongue felt warm between my legs and I moaned. His lips circled my clit and he sucked on it gently. I felt myself growing wet as he licked me eagerly. My fingers gripped the sheets as his tongue teased me.

KNOCK KNOCK.

I froze as I heard someone knocking on the door. I reached down and tugged on Tom's hair so he would stop, grateful when he paused. I lay there silently, hoping that whoever was at the door wouldn't come in.

KNOCK KNOCK.

I lay there and watched as Dominic walked through the door.

"Morning." He stood at the door in just his boxers, and I stared at him, unsmiling.

"What do you want?" I looked at him with a blank look.

"I'm sorry about what I said yesterday." He gave me a wry smile. "I was a jerk."

"Yeah, you were." I nodded in agreement.

"I reacted badly to seeing you fucking my dad." He made a face. "I'm sorry."

"It's fine," I croaked out, hoping Tom couldn't hear.

"I shouldn't have come to your room last night and said what I did after sex." His words sounded loud, and I yelped as I felt Tom's teeth nibbling on my clit. "You okay?"

"Yes." I nodded and tried to close my legs.

Unfortunately, Tom was having none of it, and his tongue was now entering my very wet pussy. Thankfully, the duvet was so thick that it would be hard for Dominic to realize that someone was in the bed with me.

"Anyways, I wanted to come and say that I hope we can talk once we get back to the city." He shrugged.

"Yeah," I muttered and tried not to moan as Tom's tongue had me on the brink of orgasm. "That's…" I closed my mouth and my fingers tightened on the sheets as I felt myself coming on Tom's face.

"I knew there was another guy." Dominic made a face. "So it's not like you lied to me. At least I knew you had another lover."

"Yup," I was able to squeak out as Tom's tongue licked me up.

"I guess I'll let you sleep." He looked put out, and I nodded.

"Bye." I gave him a small wave and watched as he walked out of the door and then closed it. I closed my eyes, lay back on the bed, and then pulled the sheets down. "What were you doing?" I glared at Tom, and he grinned at me.

"I was making you come."

"You shouldn't have done that." I groaned as he moved back up beside me.

"Why not?"

"It just... I don't know." I sighed. "Nothing." I didn't know how to tell him that it made me feel like a cheater. I felt cheap. It had felt wrong having Tom pleasure me as I spoke to Dominic.

"So you're doing the father and the son?" He looked at me for a second and lay back on the pillow.

"I have." I nodded.

"So which one am I here to irritate?" He grinned at me. "And how far are you willing to go to get them upset?"

"I don't know." I sighed. "I really don't know."

"I'm all for playing your game, Saskia," he continued, "but some of the rules have to change."

"Oh?" I frowned as I saw his expression change. "What rules?"

"We're going to do things my way." He ran his fingers through my hair. "What I say goes."

I swallowed as I looked into his eyes, but I still nodded in agreement. "Okay," I whispered. "What you say goes."

That was one of the biggest mistakes I'd made in my life. I'd always trusted Tom up until that point. I'd always thought he had my best interests at heart. I don't know why I thought that. I should have known better. All men are dogs, and at the end of the day, they all end up looking out for themselves. Agreeing to go by Tom's rules changed everything. It was the piece of the puzzle that changed the whole game.

CHAPTER SEVEN

Aiden was sitting at the table with Jessie when I went out to grab breakfast. She was one of those girls you knew was going to be a bitch before she even said one word. She looked like she thought she was perfect. I hated her on sight, of course. Both because she looked like a stuck-up bitch and because she was dating Dominic.

Dominic was supposed to be the guy who changed my life. I hadn't quite admitted that to myself, but in my subconscious, I'd known. He was the one who was meant to make me whole. He was the one who was supposed to make me believe in love again. When he'd looked into my eyes as we made love, I'd really thought, in the depths of my soul, *This is it.* I guess I'm a fool—just like everyone else.

"Good morning, Saskia." Aiden nodded at me as he drank his black coffee.

There's something wrong with people who drink their coffee black, with no milk and sugar. It tells you something about their personality. It tells you that they don't care what they have to give up to get the benefits from any situation. Be careful of people who drink their coffee black.

"Good morning." I nodded and sat down. I didn't bother giving Jessie a smile.

I can't fake being nice. Don't be so surprised at that. There's no way you thought I could. If you didn't know it by now, I can be a bit of a bitch.

"This is Jessie, my son Evan's girlfriend." He introduced us and I looked up.

She was staring at him with something akin to lust in her eyes, further proving my suspicions that something had gone down between them.

"Hello, Jexie," I said, but she didn't even look at me.

I was right—she was a bitch as well. I smiled to myself as I grabbed the orange juice. I loved putting bitches in their place. Absolutely loved it.

"Aiden, my friend Tom was in the neighborhood, so I said he could stop by. Is that okay?"

"What?" He looked at me with a frown.

He was annoyed. He didn't like me taking liberties with his time and space. This was his hour and his game and he was the only player as far as he was concerned. Idiot. That's the problem with men who have it all. They don't realize it's all an illusion. No one has it all.

"My friend, Tom, is here." I smiled at him. "I hope that's okay."

"It's not." His eyebrows furrowed, and he was about to talk again when Jessie touched his arm.

"Are you guys fucking?" she asked softly. I could hear the hurt in her voice.

Aiden looked at her for a second and then picked up his paper and started reading. I laughed internally, though I still felt ashamed of myself.

"What do you think?" I looked at her and smirked. "I mean, what did you think we were doing when you walked into the room last night?"

"Tramp." She gave me a scornful look, and I laughed.

"What's so funny?" Dominic walked into the room looking like a Greek god, and I sighed.

"Nothing, darling." Jessie stood up and kissed his cheek. "I was just saying how shameful I think it is for your dad to bring his mistress home."

"Jessie." Dominic's face froze and he gave me a quick look.

I was ashamed that my heart was jumping as he gave me a small smile. I looked away, not wanting him to think I'd forgiven him for what he'd said to me last night. I knew it had been out of anger, but still, I was hurt and I knew that his words were partially true.

"Evan, take care of your girlfriend." Aiden looked up, annoyed. "Saskia, come with me."

I looked up, feeling annoyed and angry. Normally Aiden's constant thoughts of himself and his own pleasure didn't bother me, but now that we were here in front of Dominic, I was annoyed.

"Where are you going, Dad?" Dominic asked softly.

"To do some business." Aiden grinned and stood up. He peered down at me with sparkling eyes. "Are you ready?" His voice was light, and I knew that none of this had affected him in the slightest. He really didn't care.

"I haven't eaten as yet."

"I have something for you to eat in the study," he replied swiftly, and I looked away as Jessie gasped.

"I'll be there after I have my breakfast."

"I'd rather you come now."

"Give the girl a break, Dad. If she wants to eat breakfast before doing some work, let her eat." Dominic sounded angry, and though I tried to look at him, he avoided eye contact with me.

"Don't tell me you're mad." Aiden sounded surprised.

"I just want to eat my breakfast." Dominic shrugged and poured himself some coffee.

"Excuse me." I stood up. "I just remembered I have to call my friend Natasha this morning. I'll be right back." I hurried to my room, feeling uncomfortable.

I was happy to hear the shower running as I entered. I didn't really want to have a conversation with Tom right now. Or sex. I sighed as I realized that he was possibly another complication in my life. I grabbed my phone and called Natasha.

"Hello," a deep voice answered, and I thought about hanging up.

"Is Natasha there?" I asked Brad, her annoying husband.

"She went for a run." His voice was short.

"I see."

"Who should I say was calling?" he asked stiffly, and I stuck my tongue out at the phone. Brad was such a dick.

"You know it's me, Saskia. I know that my name and photo shows up on the screen."

"Sorry. I must have missed it."

"You're such an asshole."

"And you're a self-centered bitch of a friend," he responded smoothly.

"Ask her to call me when she gets back, please." I sighed, not in the mood to take him on.

"It sounds serious."

"It is urgent that she call me back."

"Who did you fuck now?" he said softly, and the phone went silent.

Neither one of us said anything for about a minute as we waited to see if the other one was going to talk. It was awkward and uncomfortable. Part of me just wanted us to hash it out. It had been years that we'd hated each other, and Natasha just didn't understand why. I didn't know how to tell her. And I knew that he never wanted to tell her. I mean, he hated me and I hated him. We were both disgusted with each other. I sat on the bed and closed my eyes as I thought back to all those years ago.

"You're an asshole," I whispered into the phone.

"And you liked it."

"Just tell Natasha to call me."

"I don't know why she's still friends with you."

"I don't know why she's still married to you," I snapped back.

"So are you seeing anyone?" he asked softly, and I laughed.

"You don't know the half of it."

"So tell me."

"Are you joking?" I exclaimed.

"Who best to tell than the guy who knows just how low you can go?" he said softly, and I sighed.

He was right, of course. I didn't want to tell Natasha everything. She didn't know about Tom and me, and I wasn't sure how she would react if she heard that I'd been keeping it a secret for all these years.

"You're a jerk, you know that?" I sighed. "And if I choose to tell you, it's not because I like you. It's because I have no one else to tell."

"That's fine."

"Are you cheating on Natasha?" I blurted out to change the subject.

"No, never! Of course not!" he exclaimed.

"Well, not never," I muttered.

"Saskia." His voice went low. "Don't."

"I hate you."

"It was your fault," he muttered in reply.

"I was testing you and you failed."

"It wasn't supposed to go that far." He sighed. "You should have stopped."

"I know." I bit my lower lip. "I know."

"You couldn't stop though, could you?" His voice was harder now.

"No."

"I couldn't stop either," he whispered, and I froze at his tone. It reminded me of that night. The night that cemented for me that I didn't deserve happiness.

"I have to go." I quickly hung up the phone.

I stared up at the ceiling and laughed hysterically. No wonder this weekend was going so horribly. There was all sorts of bad karma waiting to come back and get me.

The Night I Seduced Brad

I didn't intentionally try to sleep with Brad. I would never do that to Natasha. I loved her like a sister. I wanted the best for her. I cared about her so much that I didn't even act upon the initial attraction I'd felt towards Brad when I'd first met him. I knew that he'd felt it too.

We were nineteen when we met. He and Natasha had only been dating for a few weeks. They hadn't even slept together yet. We'd had an instant attraction. He couldn't stop staring at me, and I couldn't stop my fingers from burning every time they brushed his on the table. We played a cat-and-mouse game all night, and I'd never felt so stimulated by a man before.

Then Natasha told me how much she liked him. How they had some classes together and he was the smartest guy in the class. She was happy and excited, and I knew that I couldn't act on my attraction. I was cold to him for the rest of the night, and while he looked confused, he didn't say anything to me about it.

About two months later, he asked Natasha to be his girlfriend (officially) and that was that.

We saw each other every other month after that, and we were cordial to each other up until the bathroom incident. Natasha and I had planned a weekend getaway to Vermont with Brad and a guy I was seeing at the time. It was to be a romantic getaway, and I was so excited to get out of the city and have some fun. Unfortunately, we ended up renting a one-bedroom cottage, so none of us had any privacy. One night, I left a note on the pillow for my date to meet me in the bathroom at midnight. We'd all been drinking that night and had invited some locals we'd met at a bar to come over and party. I grinned to myself as I slipped out of the room at 11:30 p.m. and made my way to the bathroom. I slipped my panties off and stuffed them under the sink, and then I pulled my bra off, turned the light off, and waited. As the clock struck midnight, the door opened. I giggled in the dark and pulled my date in quickly, locking the door behind me.

"I—" he started, and I put my finger to his lips.

"Shh," I whispered, enjoying the naughtiness of the moment.

I moved towards the bathtub and bent over, pulling my skirt up as I stuck my ass out. He knew exactly what to do, even in the dark. One of his hands circled my waist as the other one undid his zipper. He grunted as he rubbed the tip of his cock against me. I grinned to myself as I gripped the bathtub. I was already wet, and I knew that was turning him on even more. He wasted no time before sliding into me, and I cried out as he filled me up.

"Ooooh!" I moaned as he grabbed ahold of my hips and pulled out slowly before pushing back inside me.

"Like that, do you, Natasha?" He laughed as he slammed into me again.

I froze when I realized that I was in the bathroom with Brad and not my date.

"Oh shit." I pushed back against him and straightened up.

"What the...?" he exclaimed, and when I turned on the light, his face was pale. "Oh shit!" he exclaimed as he looked at me.

"Why are you here?" I stared at him with wide eyes, trying to ignore his gigantic, hard cock that was still standing at attention.

"Natasha left me a note..." he started and then groaned. "Oh shit, she didn't leave me a note, did she?"

"I left a note for Nick." My face reddened. "Shit."

"Oh my God." He leaned back against the door. "I didn't know."

"It's okay." I took a deep breath. "We made a mistake. Neither of us did this on purpose. It's not our fault. We stopped as soon as we realized."

"Yeah." He nodded and stared at me for a few seconds. "We did."

"I'm sorry." I sighed and walked towards him.

"It's okay." He nodded, and his eyes fell to my breasts. "It's okay."

"You should probably put that away." I nodded at his cock and laughed slightly.

"Oh, yeah." He continued staring at me.

I'm not sure what came over me then, but I reached over, grabbed his cock, and held it in my hands for a few seconds. His breath caught as I touched him, and I could feel my heart beating fast. I held him for a few more seconds before placing him back in his pants and doing up his zipper.

"Thank you." He nodded, his eyes filled with lust.

"It's okay." I stood there in front of him, barely breathing.

"You're cold?" His fingers reached up to my breasts and he lightly squeezed my nipples.

"A little." I nodded as his hands cupped my breasts.

"I thought so." His fingers continued playing with my stiff nipples and then dropped to his sides. "I should go."

"Yeah." I nodded in agreement. "You should."

"Okay."

"Don't feel bad, Brad. We didn't know and we stopped when we realized."

"Yeah." He opened the door and then stared at me for a second before leaving. "We did." He walked out of the bathroom then, and I locked the door behind him.

I would be a liar if I didn't tell you that I wished we hadn't stopped. I left the bathroom about five minutes later, and about thirty minutes after that, Brad proposed to Natasha. I wasn't sure if it was due to guilt or something he'd already planned, but I smiled and congratulated them both as if nothing had happened. I could still feel him inside me even though it had only been a few seconds.

After that, things had gotten even tenser between the two of us. We'd never really been friendly and resentment had set in as we both kept the secret of what had nearly happened that night. Though that wasn't why we now hated each other.

***

I hadn't planned on seducing Brad. I'd just wanted to test him to make sure he was going to be faithful to Natasha. I knew that the best place to find that out would be at the bachelor party.

It was easy to sneak in to the party and pretend that I was one of the dancers. I wore a long, raven wig and a mask over my face. I didn't go straight up to Brad. That would have been too easy. I danced around the room, giving his friends lap dances, and kept my mouth shut as their fingers grabbed my breasts and butt.

I was wearing a thong bikini and a small top, so I knew I was attracting a lot of attention. I noticed a few of the other dancers staring at me as I danced, but I ignored them. I knew the less I said, the better.

To be fair to Brad, I didn't see him getting many dances. He laughed and brushed the girls away as he drank his beers. I pulled one of his friends to the side and told him that I wanted to give the groom a private dance as was customary for bachelor parties. I told him to get Brad to sit down in one of the soft leather chairs and to dim the lights. Of course, the guy was happy to oblige.

The lights dimmed within minutes and the music went up. I watched as Brad sat down in the chair and grinned. This was it, then. This was the test. I wanted to see how far he'd go. I wasn't going to push it. I just wanted to make sure he was trustworthy.

I danced over to Brad and wiggled my ass in front of him. He shook his head as I wiggled my ass on his lap, but he stopped as his friends started groaning.

"You have to have one dance, Brad."

They grinned and laughed, and I watched as he shrugged and danced. He gave me a quick smile, and I started dancing again. I hadn't seen any recognition in his eyes, so I knew that he didn't know who I was.

I started the dance pretty conservatively, but soon I was writhing around in his lap to the beat of the music. I peeled my bikini top off and threw it into the crowd. Some of the guys were clapping, and I grinned at them before grabbing Brad's hands and placing them on my breasts. He was hesitant at first, but soon, he seemed to be enjoying himself, and his fingers squeezed my breasts and pinched my nipples eagerly.

I was disappointed that he was getting so into it, but I knew that I had to continue to see how far he would go. I tried to ignore the part of me that was excited to see what would happen. I didn't want to admit to myself that I was enjoying the dance as much as he was. I continued gyrating on him, and I moaned as I felt his hardness against my ass. It was almost time to see if he would stop me if I went to squeeze his cock. However, before I had time to reach behind me, I felt his hand between my legs and his fingers squeezing inside my thong.

"Oh." I froze for a second as I felt his fingers gently rubbing my clit.

"I know who you are," he whispered into my ear as his fingers played with me.

I turned around to look at him, and his eyes burned into mine.

"I don't know what game you're playing, Saskia," he whispered into my ear again, and I felt one of his fingers enter me. "I don't know why you're doing this to me."

"What are you doing?" I moaned, not wanting to stop the charade.

"I've thought about this ever since that night in Vermont," he said, groaning as he fingered me.

"Brad." I shook my head and got off of his lap. He grabbed my thong and pulled it down my legs.

"I think you need to finish your dance." He sat back in the chair and stared at me for a few seconds with hazy eyes.

And I had. I'm ashamed to admit it. I think we've both blacked out that memory. I fucked him on the chair in front of his friends and they all cheered us on. They all cheered on as if it were fine. When we'd both come, I'd gotten up and left and that had been it. We'd never spoken about that night.

I was ashamed of myself and disgusted with him. I knew that, if Natasha ever found out, it would break her heart.

I started laughing again then, loud and sad laughter. This moment with Dominic and Aiden was payback. Payback for sleeping with my best friend's husband.

"What's so funny?" Tom walked out of the bathroom, dripping wet, a towel hanging loose around his waist.

"Why did you take a shower?" I shook my head in confusion. "You just got here a few hours ago."

"I wanted to be clean when I met your friends."

"What friends?"

"Exactly." He plopped down on the bed next to me, drops of water flying from his body onto mine. "None of them are your friends."

"What's your point, Tom?"

"Why are we here?" He looked at me and raised an eyebrow. "Let me take you home."

"Tom," I groaned, worried that he was going to attempt to make a move on me. Not a 'making love' move either, but an 'I love you, so let's try and make this work' move.

"I don't understand why you—"

"No." I grabbed his arm. "Please, Tom. Not now." I sighed and rubbed my forehead. "I don't need this right now."

"Are you okay?"

"I'm fine." I sighed. "I just called Natasha."

"Oh?"

"I spoke to Brad."

"Oh." Tom made a face. "Awkward still?"

"Yeah." I sighed. "It's still awkward."

"Don't let it bum you out." He shrugged.

"I feel like I'm a horrible friend and that everything that's happened this weekend is what I deserve."

"It's not your fault." Tom's hand crept up to my breast. "You can't help it if you're a sexual creature."

"That's not what this is about," I snapped and pushed his hand away.

I stared at him as if I didn't know him. Tom had always been the guy I called to comfort me, but now I was starting to wonder if he'd ever really provided comfort. Yes, he provided sex, but maybe sex wasn't the way to make me feel better about everything. As I thought back to that night with Brad, I felt my stomach churning with guilt and pleasure.

"Don't tell me to stop," Tom hissed back at me, and I froze.

"Excuse me?" I stared at him in surprise.

"You think you're going to give it up to everyone else but me?"

"Tom!" My voice was shrill, and he sighed.

"Sorry." He jumped up and the towel fell to the bed. "This is just getting old."

"What are you saying?"

"I'm saying that if you want me to stick around, you're going to have to show me."

"What, do you want a blowjob?" I snapped. "Is that it?"

"Oh no." He turned around and smiled at me. "I want a whole lot more than that."

"Tom, it might have been a mistake bringing you here." I looked at him sadly. "I don't think this is going to work out."

"Oh?" He looked at me with sad eyes.

"You've been my best friend for years, but I don't know if this is what I want anymore. I think you need to leave."

"Are you sure about that?" His voice was harsh.

I knew that our relationship had come to the end of its road. I didn't trust Tom anymore. Not that I was the most trustworthy, but I didn't feel like he had my best interests at heart.

"Yeah, I'm sure." I nodded and got up. "I'm going into the shower. I expect you to be gone by the time I'm out."

"Okay." He ran his hands through his hair and paused. "I'm sorry, Saskia."

"Sorry about what?"

"It doesn't matter." His eyes looked sad. "Just that I'm sorry."

I walked into the bathroom then, not knowing what to say. I turned on the bath and poured some Epsom salts into the tub. I was about to step into the tub when I remembered that I had some lavender oil in my handbag. I opened the door to the bedroom and paused as I heard Tom talking.

"I'm leaving now." His voice sounded devoid of all emotion. "Yes, she seemed angry. No, I don't know. She didn't tell me. Look, don't call me again, and I expect to see the money in my account tomorrow. I did what you asked." He paused then, and I peeked into the room to see who he was talking to. I realized he was on the phone, and I quickly pulled my head back into the bathroom. "She was never mine," he said sadly and then laughed. "And contrary to what you think, she'll never be yours either." The room went silent then, and I heard the door close a few minutes later.

I peeked into the bedroom again and saw that he was gone. I wanted to run after him and ask him who he'd been talking to, but I didn't. I knew that he wouldn't tell me. He'd betrayed me and my friendship, all for some money.

I sat on the bed in shock and wondered who had contacted him and what they had wanted to know. Who wanted me that badly? It had to be Aiden or Dominic, but I didn't know which one. I didn't even know how they knew about Tom. I froze as I realized my world was unraveling around me. Everything I thought I knew, everything I'd been so certain of, was coming apart.

This is the point where you wonder who it was Tom had been speaking to. I can't tell you. Not yet. Not until you hear about everything else. You see, Tom was wrong about one thing. He'd told the person on the phone that I'd never be his. I did become his. I am his. However, becoming his wasn't the happily ever after most of you are hoping I found.

CHAPTER EIGHT

The knock on the door made me freeze. I didn't want to see Aiden or Dominic, and I sure didn't want Tom to show back up again. I needed time to think about what I'd heard. Who had told Tom to leave? There was another knock on the door, but I ignored it.

"We need to talk," she said in a shrill voice as she opened the door and entered the room.

I almost groaned when I saw Jessie. She was the last person I wanted to see.

"What do you want?" I asked her none too politely. I had no reason to hide my dislike of her.

"How dare you think that it's okay to come here and sleep with a married man?"

"Excuse me?" I stared at her with a smile on my face. "Is that any of your business?"

"I'll tell his wife." Her eyes narrowed. "And that will be the end of you."

"I don't think you will." My voice was tight as I walked towards her. "You wouldn't want to do a bitchy thing like that, would you?"

"What you're doing is not right."

"But it was okay for you?" I tilted my head and stared at her, wondering if I had the energy to give her a slap and possibly get into a catfight.

"You have no idea what you're talking about." Her eyes looked at me with a dark look.

"Does Dom—I mean Evan—know?" I smiled.

"What do you care?" It was Jessie's turn to smile at me. "I satisfy every inch of him as well." She grinned and casually lifted up her left hand. I saw a gigantic diamond ring on her finger and froze. "And now he's proposed." She smiled evilly. "So now that I'm a part of the family, I'm afraid I'm going to have to insist that you stop fucking my mother-in-law's husband."

"That's your job, right?"

"You have no idea, bitch." She took a step towards me, and I was pretty sure she was about to hit me when Dominic came into the room.

"Jessie, what are you doing in here?"

"I wanted to show Sluttier my ring." She giggled and walked back to Dominic.

"My name's Saskia." I glared at her and waited for Dominic to say something to her.

"Oops. Sorry. What did I say?" She smiled up at Dominic, and I watched as he kissed her forehead.

"Jessie, give me a moment with Saskia, please."

"Sure, honey." She reached up, gave him a long kiss, and then waved at me. "Remember what I said," she whispered before leaving the room.

Dominic closed the door behind her, and I watched as he pulled a key out of his pocket and locked it.

"It's nice to know there are locks on the doors." I rolled my eyes as he walked towards me.

"You should leave." He stopped right in front of me and frowned.

"Why? So you and your fiancée can feel better about yourselves?"

"I didn't want the weekend to go like this." He sighed.

"You wanted something else?"

"You know I wanted it to be me and you."

"Uh huh."

"I would have canceled my plans."

"Yet instead you bring your girlfriend and propose."

"It's not that simple."

"It never is."

"My parents really like her. They want to see us married. It's my dad who introduced us." His voice was pained, and I wanted to laugh.

Did he really have no clue? Was it possible that he hadn't realized that Jessie had been with his dad before him?

"I don't know what to say." I looked away from him.

"We've both made mistakes here, Saskia. I don't want to lose you."

"What do you want us to do?"

I don't even know why I asked that question. I didn't care what he wanted us to do. I wanted him to drop Jessie and tell me that he wanted to start again. That he wanted to start anew.

I told you that something must have happened to my brain. Never before in my life would I even have considered wanting to be with someone, let alone someone who had basically lied to me and cheated on me.

“I don’t know.” He made a face and reached his hand out to touch my cheek. “Right now I just want to fuck you.”

“Did you sleep with Jessie?” I asked him softly. I could tell by the look in his eyes that he had.

Now, I’m not trying to be a bitch or a hypocrite, but I wasn’t interested in being sloppy seconds, especially to someone like Jessie. Most women know what I’m talking about when I say that there are some women who just annoy the shit out of you so much that you can’t understand how or why they have friends or a man. It makes no sense.

And it burned—I’m not going to lie. It burned because I wanted Dominic. And I’d imagined him changing my life. In a way that I’d never thought I wanted, but I didn’t want him like this. It was different with Aiden. I’d known he was married when I’d met him and I’d never hoped for or wanted anything else.

“I’m going to have to ask you to leave.”

“She’s a good girl.” He shrugged. “I think you’d like her.”

"Are you serious right now?" My voice rose. Did he really think that Jessie was someone I'd ever like?

"Don't go acting like a jealous bitch, Saskia. It doesn't suit you, and frankly, it's a bit of a joke." His tone sounded arrogant and condescending, and I looked at him with hurt eyes. I couldn't believe he was talking to me like this.

"Please leave."

"But—"

He looked annoyed, and I turned away from him and waited for him to exit the room before sitting on the edge of the bed. I rested my head on my lap and just sat there for a few minutes, trying to ignore the feelings of pain thrashing around in my belly.

Then I had an idea. An idea so wicked and devious that I wondered if I could really go ahead with it.

It only took me five seconds to decide that I was definitely going ahead with it. It's funny the decisions you can make in the heat of the moment. You never think about what a domino effect one rash decision could have. My plan was to be Jessie's undoing, only it really turned out to equal mine.

The Master Plan For Jessie's Undoing

You ever have an idea that you think is so brilliant, but really it's only brilliant because you haven't thought it all the way through? I wanted Jessie out of Aiden's and Dominic's lives. My end goal was simple. I wanted Dominic to realize that Jessie was a whore (and yes, I know how ironic that sounds). I wanted for him to dump and banish her. Then I would dump Aiden and threaten to tell his wife about me and Jessie if he tried to break me and Dominic up. I was ready to be done with Aiden. He wasn't the only one who could support me, and he wasn't the one I wanted.

I had it all planned out in my head. The absolute master plan, but there was one person I needed to make it all work out. That person was Tom.

I wasn't going to tell him the plan. I knew he wouldn't go through with it if he knew what I wanted him to do. Not because he wouldn't enjoy it, but because he didn't want to help me get Dominic. I knew that, once he figured out what was going on, he would never talk to me again or at least for a very long time, but I was willing to risk it.

That was mistake number one in my plan. I didn't realize how important of a friend he was going to be until later on. Using Tom created the beginning of the end and the beginning of a new beginning for me.

I texted Tom a very short and simple text message:

Me: Meet me at the Marriott tonight at 7pm.

The lights will be out and I'll be waiting in the bed for you. Don't talk, just come and take me. I need to feel you inside of me. I miss you. I'll be in the penthouse suite.

He texted me back in two minutes with a smiley face. I laughed to myself. That had been way too easy.

Next was the hard part. I found a piece of paper and a pen and wrote: "Jessie, I've planned a romantic getaway at the Marriott tonight. In the penthouse of course! Arrive at 6:30 p.m. Put on the blindfold at the side of the bed and make sure all the lights are turned out. Take your clothes off and wait for me, naked. Also, spray yourself a few times with the perfume I bought for you. Don't talk when I enter the room. I want us to just enjoy the feelings and emotions without talking. I'll have a special present waiting for you afterwards. XOXO, me."

I decided not to put Aiden or Dominic's name in the hopes that she would just assume it was from whichever one she wanted to be with most. I folded the letter quickly and then left my room. I needed to make sure she saw the note and read it soon. But I also needed to make sure that no one else saw it. If Dominic saw the letter, everything would be ruined.

I smiled to myself when I saw that Jessie was swimming in the pool. I left the note on her towel and stood inside the living room to make sure she saw the letter when she got out of the pool. I stood there anxiously. I was worried that someone was going to come into the living room and ask me what I was doing spying on Jessie.

It wasn't like I was about to go and throw a hair dryer or something electrical in the pool. I wasn't psychotic—just a bitch.

Jessie got out of the pool in a skimpy bikini, and my eyes narrowed. I wasn't sure why she had bothered to put on anything. I could see everything but her nipples. Her thong bikini wasn't leaving much to the imagination either.

I'm not going to lie. I was slightly jealous. She had a hot body. Maybe even hotter than mine. And she was pretty hot—if you like hot, evil witches. All I could see was bitch, bitch, bitch.

I was happy that the first part of my plan was underway. I knew I had hit a homerun because Jessie's grin was huge as she read the letter. I'd never seen her look so happy. Part one had gone as planned.

Part two was just as easy. I reserved the penthouse for two nights with Aiden's American Express card before I went over and put a new bottle of my perfume next to the bed. I always wore Vera Wang's Princess, and I knew Tom would recognize the scent. I tried on the silk-lined, fur blindfold and rolled on the bed. I could see nothing and it felt sexy and sensual, just as I'd hoped.

I lay on the bed for a few seconds, grinning. This plan was going to work perfectly. I checked my watch and went down to the bar and waited. Jessie arrived as planned, right at 6:30 p.m. I pulled my phone out, waited until it turned to 6:45 p.m., and texted Dominic.

Me: Meet me at the Marriott. I'll be in the penthouse. Go to the front desk to get a key.

I sat back and waited for him to respond. My heart started racing when ten minutes passed and he still hadn't responded. Don't tell me he was going to be the wrench in the plans. Everything would be for nothing if Dominic wasn't there to witness anything. I nearly cried in relief when he texted me back about five minutes later.

"I'll be there," was all he said, but it was all I needed.

I ordered a pear martini then. I figured I could celebrate. I drank with glee when Tom arrived at 6:55 p.m. I loved that Tom was always so eager. It was a pity that the whole friends-with-benefits thing hadn't worked out, but I no longer trusted him. I still wanted to know who he had been on the phone with, but I was going to have to figure that out later.

I watched as Tom walked to the front desk to get his key. He knew the drill by now. We'd had plenty of hotel hook-ups. It killed me that I had to wait down here while the fun went on upstairs, but I pulled out my earphones, plugged them into my phone, and pulled up my Youstream account. I had hooked up my small digital video camera to face the bed so that I was live-streaming everything that was going on in the room. This was going to be good.

The screen was dark at first, but there was a little light coming in from the curtains that Jessie and I had not closed. I also noticed that there were candles burning next to the bed. My jaw dropped when I saw that there was a whip as well. I should have known that Jessie was going to come prepared. I just wish I knew who she was expecting to show up.

I'd been avoiding Aiden's texts and calls all day, and I knew that he wasn't going to be happy that I had gone rogue this weekend. This plan had to work because I knew I couldn't sleep with him again. I wanted Dominic and I was going to get him.

I stared at the screen and realized that Jessie was lying naked on top of the sheets. I'd rather she'd have been under the sheets. That way Tom would have to look and see her and know that it wasn't me. She also had a Brazilian wax, whereas I had a landing strip. I wasn't sure how much Tom paid attention to these things, but I was starting to panic again.

I watched as Tom went into the room. Jessie opened her mouth and said something, and I froze. I'd told them both to be quiet. If they spoke too much, they'd know. I frowned as I stared at the screen, not knowing what was happening and not being able to hear anything much. Tom walked across the room then and ripped off his clothes before jumping onto the bed. I couldn't see what was happening because his back filled up the screen.

That's when Dominic arrived—tall, sexy, drop-dead gorgeous Dominic. I stared at him and grinned as I pulled off my earphones and dropped a twenty on the table. I waited for him to pick up the key and then I ran to the elevator.

"Hi." I walked up to him and gave him a big kiss.

"Hi to you, too." He kissed me back passionately and ran his hands through my hair.

"I'm glad you came."

"Yeah." His hands ran down my back to my ass. "I've been thinking about fucking you for the last couple of hours. Of course I came."

"You're going to come a lot tonight." I grinned, already picturing us sharing his main room tonight. I didn't even care that he'd shared it with Jessie the day before. She was on her way out and I would soon be in my proper place.

It's funny how we can fool ourselves into believing shit when we're on a mission. Sometimes I look back and think to myself that, if I'd just gotten us a key for our own room and forgotten the plan, things could have been so much different.

I opened the door to the suite with Dominic's fingers rubbing me between my legs. I was almost upset that we had to wait to get laid, but I was too excited to be very annoyed.

"What's that?" I exclaimed in shock as I opened the door and the sounds of Jessie's moans were loud and rapid.

"Is the room occupied?" Dominic frowned and we walked in slowly.

"Maybe it's the TV?" I shrugged and grabbed his hand. "I want you so badly." I grabbed his hard cock and squeezed it before we walked in farther.

I couldn't stop grinning as I could hear the clear noises of lovemaking. Tom was grunting and Jessie was almost screaming as they fucked.

"Do me harder!" she screamed out. Her legs were wrapped around his waist and we watched as he flipped her legs up over her shoulders and started pounding her.

"Do you like that, bitch?"

"Yes!" she screamed as he moved back and forth even faster.

"What the fuck?" Dominic's voice cut through the room, and I saw Tom drop her legs and look back at us. Jessie removed her blindfold and blinked rapidly.

"Dominic!" Her voice sounded shocked.

"Jessie?" His tone was uneven, and I could see his nostrils flaring.

Jessie leaned over and turned on the bedside lamp. Her face was red and she stared at us in shock and then at Tom. Tom's expression was one of surprise and his eyes narrowed as he stared at me.

"What the fuck, Jessie?"

"I, uh…" she mumbled and bit her lip. Then she looked at Tom again. "Who the fuck are you?"

"I was sent."

"Did he send you?" she gasped. "Is he testing me?" She jumped up and ran to Dominic. "I'm sorry!" she cried and crushed herself against his chest. "I don't know that man."

Dominic frowned and gave me a small look, and I shrugged, pretending ignorance.

"Who do you think is testing you?" I looked at Jessie with an evil smile. "Aiden?"

"You bitch." Her eyes narrowed as she stared at me.

I watched as she pressed her naked body into Dominic's even harder. I could feel my face going red as I watched him stroking her back. I thought I was going to explode. This was not how this was supposed to go.

"Let me call my dad and see what the fuck is going on." Dominic went over to a chair and sat on a couch. "Who are you?" he asked Tom as he pulled his clothes on.

"You don't even wanna fucking know." Tom shook his head and ran to the door. "I hope I never see any of you fuckers again."

"That was rude." Jessie shivered and pouted as she sat next to Dominic.

"I can't believe you slept with him." Dominic stood up and looked down at her with a shocked expression.

"I thought it was..." She paused and started crying. It was then that I knew she'd been hoping it had been Aiden. I tried to stop myself from rolling my eyes and reaching over to pull her hair. "Wait." Her eyes narrowed and she looked at me. "What are you two doing here anyway?"

"Didn't you expect to see Dominic?" I asked innocently. "I mean, who did you think you were fucking with such wild abandon?"

"I need you to leave." Her voice turned cold. "Dominic, you need to tell her to leave."

Dominic looked at me and gave me a look. My blood turned cold as I realized that he wanted me to leave. I couldn't believe that he was doing this to me.

"Dominic, I thought we were going to talk." I raised my eyebrow at him. *Don't do this to me*, *Dominic*, I thought to myself. *You cannot do this to me.*

"Jessie, I have to leave. Saskia and I have to talk." He sighed. "I'll speak to you tonight."

"You're leaving?" Her eyes were wide with hurt.

"I think that's best." His tone was derisive. "We need to talk."

"I can talk now if you want..." Her words trailed off as she stared at him.

"Not now. Saskia and I have to go."

"Whatever." Jessie walked back to the bed and lay down.

I stood there for a moment feeling like I was having an out-of-body experience. This whole situation seemed surreal. Their conversation felt surreal. I really didn't understand what sort of relationship they had. I should have known at that point that something was seriously fucked up, but I guess you don't see what you don't want to see.

"So tell me, Saskia. What the fuck?" His eyes narrowed as we left the room.

"What do you mean?" I asked innocently.

"I mean exactly what I said." He grabbed my arm and pushed me against the wall. "What the fuck?"

"I don't know why you're blaming me." I shrugged.

Now you might be thinking that my plan failed. You might be thinking that it's obvious that I set everything up. At this point, that doesn't matter. That was only part one of my plan. Part two of my plan was still in progress. It still had to work out. Part two of my plan was the most important! Part two would mean the end of Dominic and Jessie. At least that was what I hoped.

Now, you have to understand that I wasn't in my right mind. Normally, I'd never do something like this. Normally, I'd just find someone else, but I felt like I had something to prove. Jessie had come into my jungle and was trying to be the lion. There was no way I was going to back down.

"How did we both end up in the room?"

"Maybe the hotel clerks messed up the reservation because the same name was used."

"You mean me and my dad?" His eyes narrowed and his breathing was hard.

"You said it, not me."

"How are you going to make this up to me?" He pulled me towards him hard.

"What do you want?" I grinned at him as he started squeezing my breasts.

"What do you think?" He grinned back.

"I think you want us to get another room." I grinned.

"Nope." He shook his head. "I don't want us to get a room."

"Oh?" I looked at him in confusion.

"Let's have some fun in the elevator."

"Hmm." I frowned. I wasn't concerned with sex in the elevator as much as I was concerned that part two might not go as planned. "Can I go and get a drink first?"

"You need a drink to fuck me?" He pressed into me so that I could feel his hardness against my stomach.

"I need a drink after all that drama." I raised an eyebrow. "I'm not used to such craziness."

"You are the craziness." He laughed and leaned down to kiss me. "Hmm, you taste so good."

"So do you." I kissed him back. "I should be offended by that."

I sucked on his tongue and ran my hands through his hair. It felt so good being with Dominic that I almost forgot how angry I was with him.

"Let's go grab that drink." He grinned. "We've got an elevator to fuck in."

I grabbed his hand and laughed as we made our way down to the bar. I excused myself, went to the bathroom, and rolled my eyes as I saw about ten angry text messages from Tom. I texted him back.

Me: She's still in the room if you want to come.

"You bitch," he replied and I grinned to myself. I had no problem with being called a bitch.

"You going back up?"

"Do I have eight inches of hardness that needs to blow a load?"

"Enjoy."

"Dirty whore."

"And I like it."

I closed my phone, sat on the toilet seat for a moment, and closed my eyes. I wasn't sure that was true anymore. I wasn't judging myself for my past, but I knew I'd made some mistakes.

I answered the phone as it rang without looking at the screen. "What do you want, dickhead?"

"Saskia?" Natasha's voice was soft.

"Oh, hey. Sorry." I made a face into the phone. "I thought you were someone else."

"Uh huh." She laughed. "Brad said you called?"

"I just wanted to say hi."

"He said you sounded upset."

"I'm surprised he could tell." I rolled my eyes.

"Saskia," she sighed. Natasha's greatest wish was for me and Brad to get on as friends.

"I'm just being honest," I huffed out. "I have to go, though."

"Okay." Her voice rose. "Call me when you're ready to talk. I'll be here."

"Thank you." I smiled into the phone. Natasha was always such a good friend to me. "I miss you."

"Let's hang out soon."

"Next weekend?"

"Yeah. Why don't you bring Tom? He can hang out with Brad."

"I didn't know they were that close."

"Oh, they play golf every week." She sounded surprised. "Tom never told you?"

"There's a lot he's never told me." My mind swirled a hundred miles a minute.

"Maybe you need to stop with Aiden, Saskia. Take a break from men."

"Are you telling me to become a lesbian?"

"No." She laughed. "Though I don't know that that would be such a bad thing."

"Natasha," I groaned.

"That's my name." She paused. "But seriously, you need to start thinking about your life and your future a bit more. You need to make some changes. Even Brad thinks so."

"What does Brad think?" I waited for Natasha to answer me, not even sure why I cared.

"He thinks you need the love of a good man. He thinks you need to get married," Natasha rushed out, and my blood boiled.

"Of course he does." I rolled my eyes.

"He said that he thinks that you need to stop fucking around and follow your heart."

"I see." I paused. "Well, I have to go."

"Call me tomorrow."

"Yeah." I hung up and texted Tom. *"Did you speak to Brad about me?"*

"Why?" he texted back immediately.

"Don't you ever talk to Brad about me again," I texted back.

"Don't worry. I'm more concerned about having that blonde bitch suck me off."

"You're going back up to the room?"

"Wasn't that your plan?"

I laughed as I turned off the phone and pushed it back into the handbag. That was my plan. It was obvious to me that Tom and Jessie would freak out once we walked into the room. They'd stop fucking and I'd look shady. However, I also knew how good Tom was in bed and I had a pretty good idea that Jessie was as open-minded when it came to sex as I was. I knew that, if Tom came back for seconds, Jessie wouldn't say no. At least I was hoping she wouldn't say no. My whole plan counted on her not saying no.

Dominic had to know that something fishy was up. There was no way around that. However, if he walked in on Jessie and Tom at it again, after being caught the first time, he couldn't blame that on anyone other than Jessie. He'd dump her ass so fast. And then I would be his one and only.

I grinned as I thought about introducing him to Brad as my man. Brad could eat cake. I left the bathroom and walked back to the table. Dominic had already ordered us two drinks.

"I left something in the room." I sighed. "I think my phone fell out of my bag."

"Okay."

"After the drinks, can we please go and get it?"

"I want to get laid."

"I'll suck you off right now if you can wait ten additional minutes to fuck me in an elevator full of people."

"On your knees, then." He grinned at me, and I heard him undoing his zipper. "Don't get up until I come."

"Demanding, aren't you?"

"That's how you like it." He nodded, indicating I should get below, and I took a quick gulp of the alcohol before getting under the table and taking him in my mouth.

I know, I know. It's demeaning. Slightly. But I didn't care. I wanted him in my mouth. I knew the power I had sucking on his cock. Even if it was under the table in a restaurant with a tablecloth hiding me. This was what I wanted and needed. This was going to help me assert my power over him. At least that's what I told myself. I didn't think that if I'd said no there would be a hundred other women willing to go under the table saying yes.

I closed my eyes as I sucked. Dominic was already hard, and I knew that he wasn't going to last long. My mind was already thinking about the look in his eyes as we'd walked into the hotel room earlier. He'd been shocked, slightly turned on, and slightly angry. I knew all he was going to be feeling was anger when he caught them in flagrante delicto again.

I was right. Dominic came quickly and I eagerly swallowed his saltiness before crawling back to my chair. I chugged the rest of my drink and jumped up.

"Let's go and get my phone." I grabbed his hand.

We walked in silence back to the elevator and then to the room. I could barely contain my excitement. This was it! My plan was going to come to fruition.

As we used our key to get back into the room, I strained my ears to see if my plan had worked.

"Oh fuck, you're so tight," Tom's voice groaned out and a spark of joy leapt up in me. *YES!* I thought to myself.

"Don't stop!" Jessie screamed out. "I'm close to coming."

"What the fuck?" Dominic's voice was loud and angry and the room went silent.

"Dominic?" Jessie's voice was shocked. "What are you… Ooh, ohhh, oh my God!" she screamed as she orgasmed.

I watched as Tom continued to fuck her for the next few seconds. I knew that he was going to make sure he came this time. He didn't care who was in the room.

"Are you okay?" I grabbed Dominic's arm and his eyes were wide with shock.

He shook his head and took a deep breath. "Find your phone. I'll be outside." He marched back through the door.

I stood there with a smile on my face.

"I'm sure you're happy." Tom glared at me as he jumped off the bed and pulled his clothes on. "It's been fun. Thanks, Gemma." He nodded down at Jessie and walked away.

"It's Jessie."

"Yeah, whatever." He shrugged and walked out of the room. "See ya." The look he gave me was one of pity.

I frowned. Who did he think he was to pity me? He was the one who'd gone back and fucked her like some sort of loser.

"You think you got the better of me, bitch?" Jessie slowly climbed out of the bed and stared at me with hatred in her eyes. "You have no idea what you've gotten yourself into, do you?" She laughed then, a long, evil laugh. "You're going to regret the day you ever decided to mess with me." She ran her hands through her hair and leaned forward, her lips next to my ear. "This is me telling you now that you've gone and messed with the wrong girl." She pulled back and walked away then.

I stood there for a few seconds, feeling jubilant, and then left the room and walked up to Dominic.

"Are you okay?" I grabbed his hand and squeezed it.

His expression was blank, and he didn't look at me or answer. I stood there for a few minutes with him in silence, wondering what was going on in his head. Had he really loved Jessie? My stomach was rumbling and my high was coming down fast. What the hell was going on? Why was he so upset? I didn't know what to think or what to do.

Now I know that I should have left. I should have run far, far away. Because Jessie had been right. I had no idea what I'd gotten myself into. I had no idea that everything was about to blow up in my face. There wasn't going to be a happy ending for Dominic and me. In fact, everything I thought I knew about him was turned upside down in a matter of days.

My whole existence was turned upside down when I found out his explosive secret. A secret that only two other people knew. A secret that ensured that my world was about to change. Dominic had never been the man I'd thought he was going to be. However, maybe that was why I was so attracted to him. Dominic was a more fucked-up version of myself.

CHAPTER NINE

Looking back, I should have realized that everything was a lot crazier than I'd thought. If I weren't so self-obsessed, I would have known. To this day, I still have nightmares about that night. It's something I can never erase from my brain. It's something that even I can't seem to get over. I never expected it, and to this day, I'm still shocked. And that's saying something. I'm never shocked. I mean, I've fucked men with other men watching. I've given blowjobs just to get into clubs. I've slept with my best friend's fiancé. I've done things that aren't acceptable. Yet I'm still shocked.

There's one thing you need to know. I could have forgiven Dominic anything. Absolutely anything, but I couldn't forgive him for this. This was too much. This took even my breath away. It's fitting in a way. It used to be that I was the one who shocked everyone. Now, there's nothing I can do that will ever be as shocking as what he did. Ironically, the day that changed everything was the day that I thought was going to be the start of something beautiful.

Do you know what betrayal feels like? It's soul sucking, pain crushing, heart breaking, and it's even worse when no one but you cares. I've never felt so alone before. How can you expect someone to feel bad for you when life blows up in your face when you were in the wrong in the first place? What's that saying? Karma's a bitch? I'm here to tell you that the saying is true. Karma *is* a bitch.

I'm going to let you in on a little secret. When I was growing up, my life wasn't that bad. It wasn't great, but it wasn't devastatingly horrible. I know most people don't want to hear that. I mean, I'm so fucked up you'd think something really bad had happened to me. I'm just jaded and I don't think I'm going to get any better.

After my little trick with Jessie and Tom, I thought I'd won. I thought Dominic was all mine and that getting rid of Aiden would be easy with a bit of blackmail about telling his wife. It's funny how things can change in an instant. I'm not even sure why I thought it would be so easy. I guess that, when you're used to having your own way, that's an easy thing to expect.

I wasn't prepared to be crushed. I wasn't prepared to be mutilated and diced into quarters. Not me physically, but my heart, of course. I could barely believe it when it went down. I can barely believe it now.

When Dominic and I left the hotel that day, we didn't go to a room to have sex. That was the first thing that shocked me. He really seemed upset at what had happened between Jessie and Tom. That had upset me. I mean, who wants to see their guy getting jealous over another girl? That should tell you exactly how much he thought about me. And yes, I know that, technically, he wasn't my guy, but try telling my teeny-weeny heart that.

You might think I'm overreacting about what happened, so I'm going to tell you step by step exactly what went down and you can let me know what you think. How would you have reacted?

The day my heart was shocked and broken

I decided to have a bath when I got back to Aiden's house. Partially because I thought Dominic might try and slip into my room for the quickie we hadn't had in the hotel. Oh, isn't it funny how we convince ourselves that everything is going to be fine when all signs point to a completely different ending?

My bath was short and unfulfilling. Dominic didn't join me, and I received a phone call from Brad. I nearly didn't answer the phone because he was the last person I wanted to talk to, but I answered just in case something had happened to Natasha.

"What?" I snapped into the phone. I was already in a bad mood.

"How are you doing?" His voice was soft, and my heart stopped.

You ever have one of those moments when you remember something from the past and you feel a slight tinge of pain and regret at how things turned out? It's usually because it makes you realize that you messed up at some point in your life. I try to live with no regrets, but how can any of us have no regrets?

"I'm fine. What's up?"

"I was thinking of you and I just wanted to make sure you were all right."

"Why do you care?"

"I don't care." His voice was bitter.

"Then don't bother calling me." I hung up then and cried.

I cried for the life of normalcy I wished I had. I cried for all of the uncertainty and unknowing. I cried because I knew that Dominic didn't love me even though I didn't want to accept or acknowledge that.

When I got out of the bath and looked in the mirror, I realized just how young I looked. My face was red and splotchy, and for the first time, I saw the very real sadness in my eyes. For the first time, I realized just how alone I was, and it scared me. I was scared with every fiber of my being. Do you know what it is to feel alone? To feel desperate? To feel as if the whole universe is going on like normal but you're somehow stuck in a void of nothingness?

When I left the bathroom, there was a letter on my bed. A beautiful, white linen sheet of paper. That should have been my first clue. What man has crisp, white linen sheets of paper lying around?

The note was simple and sweet:

My dearest,

This has been a crazy weekend. I'm so sorry you had to go through all this drama. Let me make it up to you! I want to show you how special you are to me. Please give me a chance to explain. I hope we can move on from here.

Dominic

My heart expanded with hope and a certain satisfaction.

I know what you're thinking, though. You're thinking that it was a fake note crafted by Jessie, but I knew it had been written by Dominic because I recognized his handwriting. I tried to call him to tell him that I wanted to see him, but his phone just rang. About ten minutes later, he called me back. I grabbed the phone eagerly.

"Hello?"

"I want to fuck you. You turn me on." His voice was loud.

"I want to fuck you too," I breathed into the phone.

"Get naked for me."

"Where shall I meet you?"

"Take your clothes off and let me watch."

"Okay, but where should I meet you?"

"I want you to suck my cock while he watches."

"Wait, what? Dominic?"

"You like that, don't you?" His voice was lust filled, and I was about to ask him what he was talking about when my phone died.

I had no clue what the fuck was going on, but I wasn't really thinking. I ran back to the bathroom and put on a robe over my naked body. I was going to show up with nothing on but the robe. Then I would drop it and push him down on the bed. My body shivered in anticipation. I couldn't wait.

I decided to walk to Dominic's bedroom. I was pretty sure that Jessie wasn't going to show her cheating ass back in the house. I grinned to myself as I walked hurriedly to the bedroom.

I knew as soon as I got to his door that I was in for a great night. I could hear the sounds of jazz music playing in his room, and as I opened the door, the room was dark and there were candles lit.

I opened the door and was about to call out when I heard grunts. I smiled to myself as I realized he had gotten started by himself. I opened my robe and then paused as I realized there was movement on the bed. I froze and stared in shock.

Dominic was in here fucking Jessie?

"Sit on my face, you dirty bitch!" Aiden's voice shouted into the room.

My mouth dropped in shock as my eyes adjusted to the dark. Jessie's naked body was on top of the bed, and I could see her moving slightly. She starting crying out in pleasure, and I couldn't believe what I was seeing and hearing. Poor Dominic! I couldn't believe that she and Aiden would have sex in his room.

That's when the world stopped.

"Suck my big cock, Jessie." Dominic's voice was hoarse. "Take it into your mouth further," he groaned.

I took a small step towards the bed and saw that Jessie and Aiden weren't breaking Dominic's heart. In fact, he looked like he was in absolute pleasure as Jessie sucked him off. All three of them seemed to be completely into the threesome, and I knew in my heart that this wasn't the first time it had happened.

I watched them all on the bed for a couple of minutes, and I felt as if I were frozen. What the fuck was going on here? I hurried out of the room with my eyes burning and ran back to my bedroom, stumbling over my own feet.

"Are you okay, Saskia?" Aiden's wife came out of a bedroom and looked at me with caring eyes.

"I'm…I'm fine." I looked away from her, feeling awful for her and what was going on in her house.

"You've just seen Jessie, then?" She raised an eyebrow.

"Kinda." I bit my lower lip and looked into her suddenly cold eyes.

"Stop looking sorry for me. I'm not an idiot, Saskia, and neither is Jessie. Do you think we didn't know that Dominic and Aiden brought you in to replace her?"

"Excuse me?" My voice rose and my eyes popped.

"The letter on your bed was the letter that Dominic gave Jessie a couple of years ago when she found out that he was sleeping with a different girl. I gave him the paper. It's from my special collection." She smiled at me.

"Huh?" I can tell you that, if shock could kill a person, I would have been dead then.

"Dominic and Aiden share women, Saskia. You should know that, seeing as you're one of the pieces of trash that they share."

"I, uh—"

"Don't bother trying to lie to me." She laughed and shook her diamond tennis bracelet. "Do you think you're the first girl that's been sleeping with my husband and then just happens to meet my son and start sleeping with him?"

"This has happened before?" My voice was low.

"Jessie started as Aiden's lover then started dating Dominic, and they enjoy their little romps."

"You're okay with this?"

"Don't let the sweet act fool you, darling. I have my own lovers." She smiled sweetly. "But I like Jessie.

She's the best girl we've had in this arrangement. I won't have you replacing her."

"I don't want to sleep with your hus—with Aiden anymore." I shook my head.

"Aren't you glad that we showed you what awaits you if you stuck around?"

"I don't understand."

"Neither Dominic nor Aiden really want you, Saskia. They want the power of having you and using you. They can do whatever they want to you and you do it."

"I don't do whatever they want."

"I can tell you're not into the threesome." She laughed cruelly. "Best for you to pack your bags and don't come back."

"Your whole family is sick." I shuddered.

"But we're rich." She smiled, looked at her wedding ring admiringly, and showed it to me. "This is a ten-carat diamond set on twenty-four-karat gold." She smiled as she waved it in my face. "Such a pretty ring, isn't it?"

I stared at her in shock for a while before I turned around, ran back to the room, and packed up my bags. I had to get out of this house of horrors. My mind was spinning.

Aiden and Dominic were sharing their women. Was that their plan for me as well? They wanted to share me? I shuddered as I grabbed my bags and then started giggling hysterically. Here I had been changing my whole mind-set. Here I had been falling in love. Here I had been becoming a different person. And for what? Two people that were more fucked up than I was.

I grabbed my phone and called Tom to come and pick me up, but he didn't answer. I pressed end on the phone when the voicemail came on to stop myself from crying into the phone. I didn't want him to see my weakness. I then called Natasha instead, but she didn't pick up.

"Natasha, it's Saskia. I need your help. Please call me back." I grabbed my bag and ran to the front of the house. I had just slammed the front door closed when my phone rang. It was Natasha.

"Hey, oh my God. I need your help. You will not believe what just happened."

"It's me, Saskia." The voice was deep and wry, and I realized it was Brad.

"Where's Natasha?"

"She went out and left her phone."

"Oh."

"I listened to your voicemail. Do you need help or not?" His voice was blunt.

I bit my lower lip. I needed a ride. I needed a place to stay. However, I knew that it wasn't a good idea to accept the help from Brad. I needed it to come from Natasha. I needed to be in debt to her, not anyone else's. I couldn't allow myself to accept any help from Brad. I closed my eyes and wiped the tears from my cheeks. Tears that were running without my approval.

"Okay, come and get me," I shot out and felt my heart pounding. I had no idea what I was doing, but all I knew was that I needed to get away from here, and fast.

“I’m coming.” His words were soft, and he hung up as soon as I gave him the address.

***

I know what you’re thinking. You’re thinking that I’m a bitch and a mess. You’re thinking that nothing is sacred to me. You’re thinking that accepting a ride from Brad was a horrible thing to do, given our past. You might be right. I wish I could tell you that I’d just called a cab and gone to a motel. I wish I could tell you I’d gotten my act together after seeing the ménage à trois of my nightmares, but I can’t.

This is my true diary. This is my story. I warned you that it wasn’t going to be pretty. I warned you that you might not like me. You may even hate me by the end of my story. I told you before that love isn’t all fairy tales and sugary-sweet stuff. Sometimes it’s gritty and raw. Sometimes it’s full of heartaches and pain. Sometimes love even becomes the pain.

My phone rang while I was waiting for Brad to pick me up.

“Hello?”

"It's me."

"What do you want?" My voice was low and sad.

"I want you to give me another chance."

"Whatever." I sighed. "We've been over this before."

"I love you, Saskia." Tom's voice cracked.

"No. No, you don't."

"Did you know that Natasha has her art exhibit tonight?"

"What? No?" I exclaimed.

"Yeah. Tonight's her big night and you should have been there. You're her best friend."

"I know." I hung up the phone, not wanting to hear any more, and stared at the ground as everything sank in.

The car pulled up about thirty minutes later, and I slowly got into the passenger's seat. Brad was wearing a tuxedo and a grim expression. He didn't say anything to me as he took in my disheveled appearance. I sat back, closed my eyes, and stared out of the window.

My heart was breaking inside for all of the wrong reasons. I pulled out my phone and sent a text to Tom.

"Fine. I'll give you another chance. Call me tomorrow."

I turned my phone off as soon as I sent the text and turned on the radio. "I Only Have Eyes for You" played through the speakers and I started crying.

CHAPTER TEN

When people look at me today, they think that I have the perfect life. I'm beautiful, I have enough money to be comfortable, and I have a man who loves me. They don't know the hell I've been through. They don't know the rot inside of my soul. It's so easy to look on the outside and think, 'Lucky her.' By all appearances, my life is perfect.

But appearances can be as fake as a plastic Barbie. I mean, it's true that, some days, I'm the happiest person in the world. Some days, I can forget the person I was and still am. Some days, the anxiety and the fear are but a memory, but other days…

Other days are dark and gloomy and I'm just waiting for the axe to fall. I'm just waiting for karma to catch up with me. Sometimes I think it already has.

I know the big question you want to ask. Do I feel bad about the pain I've caused? Do I regret sleeping with so many men? I should say yes, right? It would make you like me more. It would make me look like I learned from my mistakes. But that would be lying! I don't regret a single fuck! Not one.

***

"You want to talk about it?" Brad's voice was soft, as if he actually cared about how I felt.

"Nope." I continued to stare out of the window.

"Do you want to go home or to Natasha's show?"

"Shouldn't you be at the show?"

"Yes." He turned the music down. "But you're her best friend and I know that she would want me to help you. That's what she's always wanted, right? She wants us to be friends."

"Come on, Brad." I turned to look at him then. "How can we be friends?"

"I think we can." He looked at me briefly, and I stared into his blue eyes. "What happened is in the past."

"It shouldn't have happened!" I cried out. "You cheated."

"I didn't want to go through with the wedding." His voice was soft. "You know that."

"I don't want to talk about this." My voice cracked as I remembered Brad begging me to give him a chance.

I didn't want to remember that. I didn't want to remember how much fun we'd had together. There's something I didn't tell you about my night with Brad. It lasted more than one night.

"We don't have to talk about it." He turned the music back up. "I'll just take you home."

"I don't want to go home."

"I meant to my place."

"We can go to the show." I wiped my face and pat my face down. "I want to support Natasha."

"She'll be happy to see you." He drummed his fingers against the steering wheel and then spoke again. "Will your friends be happy to know you left?"

"I don't want to talk about it." I sighed. "Let's just go to the show."

I gritted my teeth. I didn't want to talk to Brad about Dominic and Aiden. I was also sad that Natasha hadn't told me that she had finally put on an art exhibit. She'd dreamed of this all her life. Even though she was a pharmacist, she'd always been an artist at heart.

"You sure you can come to the show?" Brad looked at me and frowned. "Natasha's mom and dad are there, and so is her uncle."

"Of course. I'm fine," I snapped. "Are you scared to have me around the in-laws? Scared I might say something?"

"Saskia, I wish you would." His voice dropped to a low monotone. "Maybe then we can stop living this lie."

"Stop living what lie?" I turned away from him. He couldn't seriously believe that we were meant to be together, could he?

"You know that, from the first time I met you, I've had a thing for you."

"Bradley." My voice held a warning. "That's enough."

"You can't pretend that you've never thought about what could have been." He grabbed my leg, and I froze.

"Brad, you're married to my best friend."

"That didn't stop you from fucking me, though."

"I was testing you and you failed."

"You failed the test too. No one told you to ride my cock until you came."

"Brad!" I gasped. "Stop it."

"Why?" He gave me a look. "You're not a prude. You've banged half of New York."

"So why do you still want me?"

"I want you because you're one hell of a bang." His fingers slid up my inner thighs. "I've never come so hard and so urgently before."

"This is not appropriate." I shook my head and closed my legs. That had been a mistake. I trapped his fingers next to my pussy and he rubbed me gently. "Stop." I yanked his arm away. "That's enough."

"So you do care about Natasha?" His voice changed and he looked at me with narrowed eyes.

"You were testing me?" I frowned.

"I wanted to see if you would sleep with your best friend's husband again." He pulled into the parking lot.

"So you were testing me." I shook my head and gaped at him. "I thought you were serious there for a moment." I laughed in relief and got out of the car.

"Nobody said I wasn't." He gave me a quick look before closing the door and walked into the building.

I followed behind him, walking slowly. What had he meant by his comment? I was thoroughly confused. Was he interested in me or not?

"Saskia!" Natasha ran towards me as soon as I entered the room.

"How did you know I was here?" I looked at her in surprise as she gave me a hug.

"Brad just told me." She kissed my cheek. "I'm so glad that the two of you are finally getting along."

"It just took the worst night of my life," I joked, and she paused.

"Are you okay? Do you need to talk?"

I looked around the room then and noticed how many people were there. "We can talk later." I smiled at her gratefully. "This is your night."

"Okay." She gave me another quick hug. "Come. I want you to meet my family." She grabbed my arm, and we walked across the room. "Mom, Dad, this is my best friend, Saskia."

I stared at the couple in front of me and smiled. Natasha's mom and dad smiled at me, welcoming me into their circle, and I was appreciative of their openness.

"Nice to meet you." I held my hand out and shook hands first with her mom and then her dad.

"Don't forget me." Another man ran up to the group and gave me a flirtatious smile. He appeared to be in his forties with dark hair and sparkling brown eyes.

"This is my uncle, Mark." Natasha laughed. "My dad's younger brother."

"Nice to meet you, Uncle Mark."

"Just call me Mark." He grinned as he held my hand for a few seconds too long.

"The show looks amazing." I turned to Natasha. "It's so packed in here."

"Yes, it's going better than I expected." She smiled as she nodded.

"I'm going to get a drink. Anyone else want one?" Natasha's dad asked politely, and I nodded.

"I'll come with you. I'm dying for a drink."

"Then we must make sure you get one." He grinned at me, and I realized how similar he and Mark looked. If anything, he was even more handsome and distinguished-looking with his dash of silver hair.

"Yes, we must." I laughed and grabbed ahold of his extended arm.

"So, Saskia, I've heard so much about you. I can't believe we haven't met before now." He looked at me with a gentle smile.

"Uh oh. What's Natasha been telling you?" I groaned.

"Nothing." He paused. "It's Brad that talks about you all the time."

"Oh." I looked at him in surprise and blushed. "That's surprising."

"I guess you really made an impression on him."

"I guess so." I could feel my face going red.

"Don't worry. He hasn't said anything bad about you. Rather, he's been very complimentary."

"Wow." I looked around the room and saw Brad in the corner talking on the phone and staring at us. "I didn't think he liked me much."

"What's not to like?" His eyes smiled at me, and I blushed. "By the way, feel free to call me David."

"I see where Natasha gets her friendly traits from." I laughed and he grinned.

"Her mom and I are so proud of her." His voice sounded wistful. "Makes me wish we had more kids."

"You guys didn't want more?"

"My wife never really wanted kids. I wanted to have a family the size of the Waltons."

"Night, John-boy." I laughed, and he smiled at me.

"Exactly." He sighed and turned to the bar. "What would you like to drink?"

"I'll have a vodka Sprite, please."

"So polite." He smiled at me again and placed the order.

I couldn't help but feel comfortable with David. He had all of the charm and friendliness of Natasha and he made me feel right at home. He was the sort of father I wished I'd had growing up. Someone sweet and charming. Someone who pushed me. Someone who would be proud of me. Someone who would love me.

"You okay?" David handed me my drink.

"Yes, sorry. I was just thinking."

"You're too pretty to be thinking that hard."

"Don't I wish." I laughed and drank down my drink. All of a sudden my mind was on Dominic and Aiden. What sort of sick fucks were they?

"There you are, brother." Mark's booming voice broke me out of my reverie.

"And there you are, Mark." David's voice sounded dry, and I looked up.

"My, my, who knew Natasha had such good-looking friends?" Mark looked me over and winked.

"Who knew she had such a good-looking uncle and dad?" I grinned back at him.

"You mean good-looking uncle." Mark slipped his arm around my waist, and I felt his chest against my side.

"If you say so." I smiled up at him easily.

"I do." He licked his lips slowly, and I felt him press himself against me. I didn't even flinch as I felt his hardness.

"Excuse my brother's manners. He thinks he's God's gift to women." David rolled his eyes.

"I don't just think." Mark chuckled and took a step back. "Excuse me." He bowed his head as his hand brushed against my breasts. I was pretty confident that his touch hadn't been an accident.

"Mark." David frowned and pushed his brother out of the way. "Stop being a pig."

"Stop being an old fart," Mark shot back. "I'm just trying to get to know Saskia."

"Hey." Brad approached us. "How is everyone doing?" He gave me a gentle smile, and I felt my heart flutter for one brief second.

"We're fine." I looked away from him. I didn't want to notice how blue his eyes looked or how buff his chest was. I didn't want to remember his hands squeezing my breasts or gripping my waist as he lifted me up and down on his cock.

"Good." He continued staring at me until I looked up and made eye contact with him. His face looked serious, and I felt slightly panicked. I wanted to ask him what he was thinking but I didn't dare.

"I was telling Saskia what a big admirer she had in you," David said and looked back and forth at us. "My daughter is lucky to have such a great best friend and husband."

"We both love Natasha," I beamed at David.

"It's important to have love in a marriage." David looked at Brad.

"Yes it is," Brad agreed. "I don't know if one should continue in a marriage if there isn't love."

"You two old women are boring me," Mark interrupted them. "Saskia, would you like me to show you around?"

"It's fine. I'll show her." Brad grabbed my arm. "I have to talk to you about something anyways."

"Okay." I nodded and followed him to the side of the room.

"What do you think you're playing at?" He frowned at me, and my jaw dropped at his tone.

"What?" I glared at him.

"You need to stop flirting with Mark."

"What are you talking about?"

"Don't tell me. You want to fuck him too."

"What the fuck are you talking about?" My voice rose, and he grabbed my arm. "Where are we going?"

"Just come with me." He pulled me into a dark corridor and pushed me back against the wall before he kissed me hard on the lips.

I felt his hands reach up to grab my breasts as he pushed his erection against me. I gasped against his lips, my heart thudding as he kissed me passionately. My hands weakly attempted to push him away, but I couldn't stop myself from kissing him back. He tasted so good. Felt so hot and hard.

His fingers slipped up under my shirt and he pulled the cup of my bra down so he could pinch my nipple. I closed my eyes at his touch and tried to banish the guilt from my mind. His fingers slipped lower, and I felt his fingers slip into my panties before he started to rub my clit. My panties grew wet, and he groaned against my lips.

"I want to fuck you so badly," he groaned, and it was as if something had hit me in the head.

I pushed him away from me with all my might and we both stood there staring at each other, gasping for air.

"What are you doing?" I groaned and adjusted my bra.

"What we both wanted to happen." He shrugged, and I watched as he sucked on his fingers.

"Don't." I shook my head. "We can't do this. You're my best friend's husband."

"I want to be with you, Saskia." He took a step towards me. "I want to make love to you. I want to be with you."

"You know that's never going to happen." I pushed him away from me. "Stop this craziness, Brad."

"You can't tell me you don't want to be with me."

"I don't want to be with you." I bit my lower lip. "Stop it," I breathed out as he grabbed my hands and pushed them against his crotch. He was harder than before, and he squeezed my fingers together so I could feel him properly.

"You see what you do to me."

"This is wrong." My hands grabbed ahold of him and I sighed.

"I want to eat you out and then fuck you hard," he whispered in my ear. "Meet me in the bathroom tonight."

"I can't." I shook my head and grabbed my hands back. "I have to go back and find Natasha."

"Think about it, Saskia." His voice was hoarse. "I'll be waiting for you. We can make this work. We can be together if that's what we both want."

I hurried back into the room and raced over to the bar. I needed another drink. And fast. Then my phone rang.

"Hello," I gasped into the phone, not even looking at the screen.

"Where are you?" Dominic's voice was distant.

"I left."

"Where did you go?"

"Why do you care?"

"Saskia, we need to talk."

"I know about you and your dad and Jessie."

"Saskia." He paused. "It's not what you think?"

"I saw you, Dominic."

"It's over," he rushed out. "Let me see you."

"You can't be serious." My voice expressed my disdain for him.

"We can be together, Saskia."

"You're a sick fuck, Dominic."

"Let me make this up to you," he pleaded. "You know the connection we had."

"Dominic, do you really think I'm going to fuck you and your dad?"

"Why not? It's not like you haven't already." He sounded bitter.

"Don't call me again." I hung up the phone and sighed. Could this day get any worse?

Mark walked up to me and smiled. "Want a drink?"

"I won't say no." I smiled at him gratefully.

"It's been a long day for you, huh?"

"You can say that again."

"It's been a long day for you, huh?" he repeated, and we both laughed.

"Something like that."

"Let me get you something stiff." His eyes darkened as he looked at me and leaned towards me. "What would you like?"

"I'm not sure." I shrugged, not bothering to move away from him as he moved closer to me.

"I think I know." He grinned and brought his hands up to the bar.

"Oh?" I raised an eyebrow at him.

"Yes, I know." His fingers moved forward deliberately, and I felt them brush over my nipples. "They're hard as rocks." He smiled at me as he pulled his fingers away. "I think you're in need of a good fuck."

"Is that right?" I stood my ground and stared at him with a small smile.

I'm not going to lie. I was horny as hell and Mark was hot. And he was a better option for me than Brad. Though I wasn't sure that there was a man whose cock could do what Brad's did to me.

"Yes." He grinned back at me and gasped as I reached down and squeezed him through his pants. He was hard and reasonably sized. Though he didn't feel as hard and big as Brad.

"Are you staying at Natasha's tonight?" I whispered in his ear, and he nodded eagerly. "Then meet me in the bathroom later." I grinned at him and then walked away.

I knew I was playing with fire. I knew that there was a chance that I'd end up fucking Brad, but part of me didn't care. I was playing a reckless game of Russian Roulette. I was going to fuck someone tonight. Be it Brad or Mark. I knew that I should have told Mark to meet me somewhere else, but I was feeling reckless.

Dominic's call had made me angry, and I knew that I was doing this to hurt him as well. I'd really thought that Dominic and I could have had a future, but he'd been even more screwed up than me. Part of me felt like I had something to prove.

I stared at Natasha across the room, who was smiling at someone, and my heart broke. I couldn't do this to her. I couldn't act on my feelings for Brad. I couldn't break her heart. She deserved better than that. I looked around the room so I could tell Mark to meet me in my room instead.

"Looking for someone?" David appeared at my side and gave me a smile.

"Have you seen Mark?" I asked him slightly urgently.

"Not recently. Why?" He frowned and looked at my face. "Are you all right, my dear?"

"I'm fine." I nodded. "It's just been a long day."

"I'm sorry to hear that." He put his arm around my shoulder and rubbed my back. "It'll get better, I promise." He smiled down at me.

I smiled back, feeling instantly comforted.

"So, Saskia, I'm going to ask you something." His expression changed slightly. "I hope you don't find it intrusive, but I have to ask."

"Go ahead." I nodded up at him.

"Have you ever been intimate with Brad?" His voice was soft, and I could feel his eyes on me. "I hope you don't think I'm prying, but..."

"Why do you think that?" I frowned at him.

"I see the way he looks at you." He shrugged. "And I know he and Natasha have been having problems."

"I didn't know they were having problems." I bit my lower lip. "It's not because of me."

"Sexual attraction can be a funny thing." He sighed. "I love my daughter and I want the best for her, but I want her to be with a man that loves her."

"Yes, I understand." I nodded and swallowed hard. "Brad and I haven't done anything since they have been married." I said, being half honest.

"I don't know why you wanted Mark, but I wouldn't look to..." He cut himself off and shook his head. "Forgive me. This isn't any of my business."

"It's fine." I nodded.

"I know this may sound crass, but a woman of your beauty doesn't have to settle for these losers."

"It's not crass." I shrugged. "I'm not going to lie. I like getting laid." I gave him a look. "Sorry."

"Don't be sorry." He offered me his drink. "There aren't enough honest people like you in the world anymore."

"Tell me about it." I laughed.

"Look, my brother Mark isn't the best guy in the world, but if you're just looking for a good time, I think he can give you what you want."

"Thanks." I laughed, feeling very awkward to be having this conversation with Natasha's dad.

"I'll tell you what." He grinned. "I'll go and find Mark and tell him you want to talk to him, yeah?"

"Yeah. That would be good." I smiled at him. "Thanks, David."

"No worries." He rubbed my back. "And don't worry. This will stay between us."

"Thanks." I kissed his cheek and then watched as he walked away from me.

***

We all left the exhibit before I had a chance to tell Mark of the change of plan. By the time we got back to Natasha's house, I didn't know what to do. I felt Brad's eyes on me all night, and all I could think about was the night we had spent together. I closed my eyes on the car ride back and decided that I was going to let the night play out however it was supposed to.

I know you're thinking what a bitch I am. How can I even think about being with Brad? My best friend's husband. When I look back, I can't say that I'm proud of myself. I can't say that I think I'm a good person. I can't say that I haven't wondered what would have been different in my life if I'd told Mark to meet me in my bedroom. But life never seems to go as planned. I know what you're thinking. But you're wrong. I swear that you're wrong.

The night that changed everything

I waited until two a.m. to get out of bed to go to the bathroom. I was wearing a long T-shirt and nothing else. I walked to the bathroom quietly, not wanting to wake anyone up. I figured I would wait for fifteen minutes and then go back to bed if no one else showed up. Part of me hoped that no one would show up.

I opened the door, walked in, and kept the light off. I sat on the bathtub, wondering what I was doing. I closed my eyes and tried to get myself to leave. Did I really want to go down this road? Part of me didn't, but the other part of me wanted my happy ever after. I wanted true love. I admit it. I was tired. I wanted someone who wanted me. Even if I had to pay the ultimate price.

After about ten minutes, I stood up and was about to leave the room when someone walked in quickly and I heard the door lock behind me.

"Where were you going?" a deep voice whispered in my ear.

My brain clicked over as I tried to place the voice. I couldn't tell if it was Brad or Mark.

"I didn't know if you were going to come," I whispered, and I felt his hands pull me towards him. "I don't know—" I started again, and I felt his fingers against my lips.

"Shh," he whispered as his fingers pulled up the back of my T-shirt and caressed my ass.

I bit my lower lip as my hands reached up to touch his face. Part of me thought it was Brad, but the other part of me thought it was Mark. Then his fingers slipped between my legs and I stopped thinking about it.

He pushed me forward until my legs hit the bathtub. I leaned forward and pushed my ass back. He groaned in response, and I felt him lean over. I cried out as I felt his lips running up and down along my slit.

"Oh!" I cried out as his tongue entered me.

I gripped the bathtub and tried not to shudder too much as I felt myself coming on his face. I was so horny that I couldn't stop myself. After about five minutes, he stood back up, grabbed my hips, and pushed me back. I felt the tip of his cock rubbing against me, and I pushed back against him. He didn't disappoint me, and I felt him entering me quickly. He thrust into me with such force that I fell forward slightly. His grip on my hips tightened and he pulled me back up without stopping his movements. His hands left my hips, and I felt him reach forward to rub my clit as he entered me. I felt my legs trembling as a second climax approached.

"Oh, I'm going to come again!" I moaned, wanting whoever I was with to speak again.

He didn't speak. Instead, he increased the force of his thrusts. My body felt like it was on fire and I thought I was going to burst.

It was then that we heard the door opening.

"Shit!" he exclaimed. "That fucking door." He groaned as he kept moving.

The light came on then and he pulled out of me. We both turned around, and there stood Natasha, standing with a pale, white face.

"Oh!" Her eyes looked at me in shock.

I felt the blood drain out of my face and then looked to my right to see who I'd been fucking. My eyes widened in distress as he gave me a small, serious smile. I literally felt like my heart was going to stop beating in that second.

"Oh!" Natasha spoke again, and her hand flew to her mouth as she stepped back.

"I…" I started and then stopped. I had no idea what to say.

I didn't know how I was going to get out of this one. I stared at him again, and I couldn't stop my stomach from flipping over as I recalled what we'd just been doing. I knew then that everything in my life was about to change. I'd gone and screwed up to the point of no return this time.

CHAPTER ELEVEN

So I broke up a marriage. It doesn't sound nice to say that out-loud, but I figured I could tell you because we're friends. Kind of. Okay, maybe we're not friends. But I lost my best friend. It still stings. I still feel bad. When I'm in bed at night lying next to my husband, I sometimes wonder if it was worth it. Was love worth it? Because we do have love. In our own messed up way. He loves me. I think it was love at first site. At least that's what he says. He tries to convince me, Though, I still don't know. This wasn't how I expected my fairy tale to go. I guess I should go back to that night. The night in the bathroom. The night that led to the beginning and the end.

"What the fuck is going on here?" Natasha's voice was harsh and her eyes were cold as she stared at me.

"It's not what you think." My voice was low as I stared at her, feeling ashamed.

"Really?" Her eyes narrowed as she stared at me. "I knew you were a slut, but I never thought you'd do this to me."

"I didn't know, I..." I paused. What could I say? I didn't know I was fucking your dad? I thought I was fucking your husband.

"Get out." She moved forward and pushed me into the bathroom.

"What?" My eyes popped open.

"I said get out," she screamed.

"Natasha," David spoke up and she turned towards him.

"How could you, Dad?" Her voice rose. "How could you do this to Mom?"

"Natasha, this isn't something that..."

"Shut up," she screamed and then looked at both of us in disgust. "I want you both to leave. I don't care where you go. I don't care what you do, but I want you both out." She shook her head and stared at me. "I always knew you had problems, Saskia, but I never thought you'd go this low."

"Natasha, your mom is going to wonder what happened if I leave." David's voice was low.

"Do you want me to tell her you left because I caught you fucking my best friend in the bathroom?"

"Calm down, Natasha, you know your mom and I haven't been happy in a long time."

"How convenient." She stepped back. "Leave now or I'm going to scream and wake everyone up."

"Natasha, please." I stepped towards her and grabbed her arm. She gave me such a look of hate that I flinched. My insides felt like they were on fire. And then Brad walked out of the bedroom in a pair of navy blue boxer shorts and no shirt and everything went quiet.

"What's going on?" He looked directly at me and then at David and Natasha. "Saskia?"

I stared into his eyes then and I could see the confusion. I waited to see the disgust. I needed to see the disgust. I needed to see that he hated me. I needed him to think I wasn't good enough. I stared and waited, but all I could see was a question.

"I caught Saskia and Dad in the bathroom." Natasha walked over to Brad and I could see tears running down her face. "I can't believe this." She started sobbing and Brad wrapped his arms around her.

"I'm sorry, Natasha. It's not what..." I started and stopped. What was the point? What could I say that would make any of it better? I looked at David and he was adjusting himself. I shuddered at the thought of him inside of me. I felt ashamed of myself as well because a part of me wanted to go back into the bathroom and continue. I knew then that I had to leave. I was so confused, so sex-crazed. That moment made me realize that I couldn't continue living my life that way anymore. I couldn't continue allowing my body to dictate my life. What was sex at the end of the day? What was my life if all I cared about was sex?

"Leave," Natasha sobbed. "Just leave."

Brad looked at me and nodded and I ran to my room and grabbed my clothes. I took a couple of deep breaths and pulled them on.

"Wanna talk?" His voice was soft as he walked into the room and I stared at him in shock.

"You shouldn't be here." I shook my head as I turned around to face Brad.

"Natasha asked me to make sure you left promptly." He shrugged. "I'm sorry."

"Why are you sorry? I'm the slut, right?" My voice rose and I looked away from him.

"I've been meaning to fix the bathroom door for ages. Every time David comes over, he tells me don't forget to fix the door." He sighed and walked towards me. "Did you think it was me?" His eyes bore into mine and I looked down. "Saskia, answer me."

"I'm not talking about this." I looked up at him angrily. "I'm not going to..."

"He's a pig." Brad's eyes narrowed and he grabbed my face. "He's cheated on her mom so many times."

"I enjoyed it." I stared at him, my heart breaking as his eyes turned bleak.

"You never did want to make this easy, did you?"

"Make what easy?" I shook my head. "It would never be easy, Brad."

"I love you, you know that, right?"

"You don't love me." I pulled away from him.

"I love you. Even though I know you've just been with him, I forgive you."

"I don't need your forgiveness."

"I forgive you, Saskia. It doesn't have to be like this."

"It has to be."

"Saskia." He grabbed my hands. "Please."

"Brad." I could feel myself getting angry. "No, no, no. I can't do that to Natasha."

"It's always been you."

"No." I felt a tear fall. "No."

"Do you remember?" he whispered.

"I remember." I nodded and looked at him.

The Day Brad Made Me A Promise

"How many times are we going to come to this park?" I sighed as we sat on the park bench.

"Until you tell me you want to date me." He shrugged.

"You're dating my best friend." I rolled my eyes at him.

"We're not dating. We've been on two dates. Shit, we haven't even slept together, Saskia."

"You need to stop asking me out, Brad."

"Then you need to stop coming to the park with me."

"I know." I closed my eyes. "Why are we doing this?"

"I don't know. Why won't you go out with me?"

"She's my best friend. I could never do that to her. There's a ho code, just like there's a bro code."

"You said ho code." He laughed.

"You know what I mean."

"Want to throw the Frisbee?"

"Not today." I shook my head.

"Feed the ducks?"

"No."

"Go to the swings."

"No."

"Make out."

"No. Wait, what? Brad." I slapped him in the arm.

"What? I had to try."

"Let's go walk." I jumped up. "We can look at the puppies."

"I'd rather look at you." His blue eyes sparkled and he looked at me with a boyish grin.

"Uh huh." My stomach flip-flopped.

"Do you know that I thought you were the most beautiful girl in the world the moment I saw you?"

"Natasha." I said simply.

"If I had met you before Natasha, would you have dated me?"

"Not going to answer."

"You always treat me so mean. I don't know why I like you." He bent down and picked up a rock and threw it.

"I don't know either."

"I like you because you're cute and funny and you don't act like I'm God's gift to women."

"That's because you're not."

"Natasha thinks I am."

"That's why you're dating her."

"I don't want to sleep with her because I don't want to cheat on you."

"Brad." I pushed him. "We're never going to be together, okay? You're nineteen. Get some while you can."

"Saskia, listen to me." He grabbed my hands. "Look at me." His eyes were serious then. "If you ever change your mind, ever. No matter where I am. Who I'm with. I'll drop everything. Just to be with you."

"Brad," I started to say, but stopped as he shook his head.

"No matter what, Saskia. I promise you I will drop everything to be with you." He pulled me towards him and I stared up into his eyes with my heart in my throat. "I know you don't want to hear it or believe it. I know I've most probably scared you, but that's a promise I make to you with everything I am. No matter what, no matter when. I'm yours. You just have to say the word."

"Okay." I leaned forward then and gave him one small, gentle kiss. We stared at each other for a few more minutes and then we went to feed the ducks. I never went to the park with Brad after that day. I started sleeping with my economics professor a few days later and Natasha told me Brad finally slept with her. We never spoke about the day again, though I had always carried it in my heart.

***

I stared at Brad in the bedroom with tears in my eyes. "I can't deal with this now. I have to leave. I've already broken Natasha's heart once tonight."

"What about my heart, Saskia?" His voice was soft and I pretended I didn't hear him.

"I'm leaving." I pushed past him.

"Do you need a ride?" He grabbed my arm.

"No." I shook my head and ran out of the room and to the front door.

"Saskia." David was waiting for me by the door.

"What?" I glared at him, my heart thumping as I imagined him inside of me.

"I'm sorry."

"It doesn't matter. Why is everyone fucking telling me they're sorry?" I shouted. "I knew it was you."

"What?" His eyes narrowed.

"I didn't know for sure, but I was pretty sure. You moved differently than Brad," I hissed. "You felt different."

"So you liked it?" He smiled and moved closer to me.

"I'm leaving." I opened the door quickly and ran out into the street quickly. I didn't know what to think or feel. Everything in my life was crashing down on me. I didn't know what side was up and what side was down. I couldn't breathe. The tears streamed down my face and I couldn't stop them. I didn't know where to go. I didn't want to go back to my apartment. It wasn't mine and I didn't want to see Aiden. I didn't want to call Tom after everything that had happened. Dominic sickened me and Brad was married to my best friend. The best friend who now hated me. I didn't have anyone. I didn't have anything.

Then my phone started ringing and I threw it into the road. There was no one who I wanted to talk to. It's funny how life goes, isn't it? Who would have thought I'd go from flying high to living in the trenches? I suppose that's karma, isn't it? I suppose you're not shocked. Some of you might even be thinking, that's what you get, bitch. Keep your legs shut. It's not something I haven't thought before. I guess you're wondering where I went, right? Did I call up one of my many men? Did I go looking for another one night stand? I'm not going to lie. I thought about going to a bar. I thought about finding a hot Wall

Street guy and letting him take me home. I even walked by a few bars in the village, but then I decided to just go home. Yes, it was technically Aiden's apartment, but I knew he wasn't about to come over. So I just went home. I've got to tell you that sleeping in my own bed felt like heaven. Absolute heaven. I cried for about two days straight. I tried calling Natasha about ten times, but she never answered.

I won't bore you with the details of the next few weeks. They consisted of me lying in bed, watching TV and eating junk food. I gained at least ten pounds. And then I started feeling sick. Every morning. And then the sick feeling started turning to actually throwing up. And then I realized that my weight gain might not be due to junk food. So I went to the bodega on the corner and I got a pregnancy test and pissed on it.

You already know the answer of what the test result said. How could you not? Don't pretend like you're shocked or appalled. Where else was my lifestyle going to lead me? However, I'm not you. I was blown away by the results of the test.

After I waited for a few minutes, I stared at the pregnancy test in shock. I sat down on the edge of the bathtub and closed my eyes. I had no idea what I was going to do. I was pregnant and I had no idea who the father was.

Then I heard a knock on the front door. I got up slowly and walked through the apartment in a daze before opening the door. I didn't even blink when I saw him standing there. It was as if I was immune to everything. Nothing was out of the ordinary anymore.

"Hi," he said softly.

"Hi," I whispered back, staring at him with wide eyes.

"What's wrong?" He frowned and I wanted to laugh. How could he ask me what's wrong so casually? After everything that had happened?

"I'm pregnant." I stared into his eyes, bleakly. I didn't care if he knew.

"Then it's a good thing that I came over, then." He stepped into the apartment and shut the door.

"I don't know if it's yours." I gave him a wry smile and took a step back. He started laughing and I looked at him oddly. He wasn't reacting the way I expected him to.

"It doesn't matter. I want to be with you, Saskia. I know that as sure as I know my own name." He grabbed me around the waist and pulled me towards him. I could feel his hardness pressing against my stomach and I swallowed hard. I didn't know if I wanted to be with him, but I wasn't sure I had much of a choice. Now that I was pregnant, everything felt different.

"Then come inside." I grabbed his hand and led him to the bedroom.

There's one thing you should know. He's not the one I ended up with. To this day, my husband doesn't know about that night. I'm not sure I can ever tell him. It's something I hold deep inside of me. It's something that I think of when I feel cold and lonely. It's something I think about when I look at my son. Because yes, my husband is not my son's father. There's one secret you still don't know.

CHAPTER TWELVE

"Brad, you shouldn't be here." I bit my lower lip as I let him into the apartment.

"I had to see you." He ran his hands through my hair.

"You should go." I shook my head, but I didn't move.

"I'll go if you want me to," he paused, "but I need you to give me one more night first."

"You know I can't do that." I shook my head and stared at him. "Please, Brad."

"One more night and if you feel the same, I'll move on." He grabbed my hands and pulled me towards him.

"You said that before." I looked into his eyes and he frowned.

"That doesn't count." He leaned forward and kissed me.

"Why doesn't it count?"

"You know why." His teeth nibbled my lower lip softly. "Just give me one more night."

"Brad." I groaned and closed my eyes.

There's something I didn't tell you about earlier. I didn't want you to judge me. I know, I know. It's a bit late for that. I didn't tell you because I'm ashamed of myself. Because I didn't stick to my own rules. I had promised myself after I slept with Brad at the bachelor party that I wouldn't sleep with him again. I'd told myself I would never sleep with him once Natasha married him. But there was one night; there was one night that something crazy happened.

The Night I will Never Forget

First thing you should know is that it wasn't my idea. I didn't even know what was going to happen until I arrived at the hotel room. And then, well, how was I supposed to say no?

Saskia,

Meet me at the W hotel. Go up to the penthouse. I have a surprise for you!

Tom

I can still remember the text message like it was yesterday. I went, of course. Sex with Tom was a welcome pleasure. We were both as open and as flexible as we could be for each other. That's what made our situation work so well. Neither one of us felt like we were being used by the other. I caught a cab to the W eagerly. I remember that I'd been having a bad day. Some bills had come due and I didn't have the money. This was before Aiden had become my sugar daddy. Because you and I both know that's a more apt name than boyfriend was.

I walked into the suite feeling excited and slightly tired. I yawned slowly as I entered, but quickly stopped still in shock. There were hundreds of candles lit around the room and all the lights were off. There was music playing on the speaker and I could see Tom standing on the balcony with his back to me.

"Hi," I whispered breathlessly, walking over to him quickly. "What have you done?" I tapped him on the shoulder and he turned around. "Oh." The blood drained from my face as I saw Brad. "You."

"Hi, yourself." He smiled at me gently. "Look at the view, it's gorgeous, isn't it?"

"It's a million-dollar view," I agreed softly, though my insides were raging. What was Brad doing here?

"I love New York," he said.

"It's a beautiful city."

"Not as beautiful as you."

"Brad, what are you doing here?" I finally bit out, excited and scared at the same time.

"I wanted a night with you."

"So Tom sent a text message for you?" I sighed, angry.

"No." Brad shook his head and looked into the room. "He sent a text for himself."

"What?" I frowned, confused.

"He said, I sent the text for myself." Tom walked towards the balcony, shirtless.

"What's going on here?" I looked back and forth at the two men and my heart started beating fast. "You guys have me confused."

"We wanted to give you a special night." Tom smiled at me and gave me a kiss on the cheek. "We wanted to make you feel special."

"Special?" I looked at him with narrowed eyes. "How?"

"We want to give you a night you will never forget," Brad whispered in my ear. I could feel the tip of his tongue licking me.

"What does that mean?"

"We want to please you, Saskia." Tom kissed my neck.

"You mean a threesome?" My voice rose in shock.

"No." Tom laughed. "We have no interest in doing stuff with each other. We just want to please you."

"Both of you?" My jaw dropped and I stared at them in shock. "No way—you've got to be joking."

"Think of it as an adventure." Brad's hand crept to my ass. "A sexy, totally awesome adventure."

"I don't know." I nibbled on my lower lip. My senses were running amok and I wasn't sure what to do. My body wanted this. This was sending my nerve endings on fire. This was something my body didn't even know that it craved.

"Come on, Saskia." Tom's fingers grazed my breast. "Just imagine, both of us pleasing you, doing whatever you wanted. Our only goal is to satisfy you."

I'm going to stop there for a minute. What would you have done? It's easy to say you would just walk away. It's so easy to say. But think about it. You're slightly tired. You're horny. Two gorgeous men want to devour your body. It wasn't an easy decision for me to make, either. Trust me. I did feel guilty. I did think of Natasha. I wanted to say no so badly. I wanted to slap them for thinking I'd even be interested. I wanted to scream. I wanted to run away. I wanted to do so many things, but I didn't. There was something about the situation. Both men touching me. Both men showing me how much they wanted me. Both men making me feel so alive in every fiber of my being. My body took over then. It completely took over my brain. Pleasure and the expectation of even more pleasure to come made up my mind. I didn't even know how it was going to work. I didn't even ask.

Brad took one of my hands and Tom took the other and they led me to the big king-sized bed. Brad pushed me down and got down next to me. I felt his lips on mine and I kissed him back eagerly. He was like water to my dehydrated body. It wasn't until he kissed me that I remembered all those forgotten kisses. I grabbed his hair and ran my fingers though it roughly, pulling at the ends. I wanted to hurt him for doing this to me. I wanted him to feel pain for making me want him. He kissed me back passionately, his tongue slipping into my mouth with ease. My fingers ran to his back and I ran them up and down, needing to taste him, wanting to erase the guilt that was already starting to build up inside of me.

Then I felt my pants being pulled down. I didn't think anything of it until I felt the cool air against me as my panties were pulled down as well. Brad shifted to the side as he kissed me and I moaned, not wanting him to pull away completely. That's when Tom's tongue met my clit. My body arched at his touch as he started licking me while Brad continued kissing me. It was as if they were in some sort of sync, as their tongues moved in and out of two different parts of my body. I cried out when Tom entered me, his tongue diving into my wetness with ease. It felt surreal to be experiencing so much pleasure at one time. I'm not going to lie, it was divine. Absolutely divine. My body started trembling as Tom's tongue brought me close to orgasm. Brad pulled back and pulled up my top and quickly unclasped my bra. My breasts lay there in excited anticipation and Brad did not disappoint. His mouth descended on one nipple as his fingers played with the other. This, all while Tom continued to eat me as though I were a five-course gourmet meal. I came quickly, my body shaking as Tom licked my juices clean. I wasn't even sure what happened next, it all seems a bit of a blur. I remember Brad moving down and pulling out his hardness, rubbing it against my clit before entering me hard and fast. I cried out as he fucked me hard. This time it was Tom's turn to fondle my breasts and he sucked on them eagerly, enjoying the look of complete and utter pleasure on my face. There is only one moment that I look back on and squirm. It's the one moment that made me feel like an object, more than a woman to be desired. It's that moment that has stopped me from doing anything similar.

Brad fucked me hard and fast and came in me pretty quickly. My body felt spent from his fucking and I was smiling like a Cheshire cat. But then, then Tom rolled me over onto my knees and entered me. This was a minute after Brad had come inside of me. Tom entered me smoothly and gently, increasing his pace after about a minute. He reached around and rubbed my clit as he fucked me. It felt crazy, wonderful, mind-blowing. His cock was slightly thicker than Brad's and he moved differently. But I remember thinking to myself, they are taking turns with me. One guy just fucked me and the other one didn't even wait. And I remember staring at Brad's face as he watched Tom fucking me. He looked hurt and I felt like a tramp because I was loving it. I screamed with Tom. My orgasm was more intense and I screamed loudly, gripping the sheets as I backed my ass back into him, so I could feel him deeper.

We all left pretty quickly after Tom came. It wasn't romantic and sweet. We didn't shower together. We didn't share a bed together and cuddle. We didn't talk about becoming one of those couples where they both loved me. We basically had sex and left. And when I left, I cried. I felt used. I felt like a tramp. And I felt like I'd let myself and Natasha down.

I've never talked about that night and neither has Brad or Tom. It's like we all wanted to forget it.

***

But now here he was, in front of me and he wanted one more night. I knew that he wanted one more night so that I could erase the memory of the ménage. He wanted me to remember him as more loving, more caring. He wanted to make me feel more special than I did.

"Brad, you shouldn't be here."

"I know you won't marry me." He sighed. "I know I'm not the father of your baby. I know you're never going to give me a chance. So just give me one more night."

"It wouldn't be right." I shook my head.

"My loving you all these years hasn't been right." He looked me in the eye. "But I've had to live with it."

"Brad, please." I looked away from him.

"I always hoped you would be mine. All these years I hoped. Tom always told me, no Brad, give it up, she'll never be mine and she'll never be yours and I never wanted to believe him. I always thought there would be a day where we would get to be together. I still want that, but I don't think you do."

"Brad, it's not about what I want." I reached out and rubbed his shoulder. "It would never work out for us. It's too complicated. We'd break Natasha's heart."

"I should have dumped her in the beginning." He sighed. "Maybe then I would have had a real shot."

"Brad, the past is the past." I reached up and touched his face. That was a mistake. I shouldn't have touched his face.

"The only mistake is me not fighting for you."

"Brad." I sighed. "Please."

"I'm not going to give up. Not until you're married and I know I have no chance left."

"Brad, you should go home."

"Being with you feels like home."

"You're determined to make this hard, aren't you? Don't give Natasha another reason to hate me."

"Why do you think of her before me?"

"She's my best friend. She has always been there for me."

"She's telling her mom, you know."

"What!" I exclaimed in shock.

"Yeah, I think David had been after a divorce for a while, if I'm being honest. He won't be able to survive by himself, though. He needs her." He shrugged. "But better men than him have fucked up."

"Who, you?"

"I'd fuck up again if I had to." He smiled and pulled me towards him. "Give me a reason to fuck up again, Saskia."

"Brad." I sighed as I leaned into him. "Why do you always make this so hard?"

"Because I love you."

"Why do you love me?"

"Because you're beautiful."

"That's not a good reason."

"It's a reason, though."

"We can't do this," I whispered as he kissed me. We kissed passionately, each of us losing ourselves in the other. I felt his hands on my breasts and I unzipped his pants. We consumed each other as if this were to be our last meal and we wanted to taste every last drop.

"Hold on." He pulled away slightly. "I'm going to the restroom. I'll be right back." He walked away from me and I sighed. How was I ever going to stop this cycle?

My phone rang as soon as Brad walked into the bathroom. I saw the number and I wasn't going to pick up, but something inside of me told me this was my out.

"Hey, you." His voice was deep and full of sorrow.

"Hey," I replied, not knowing what to say.

"Marry me," he said softly.

"What?" I gasped, not sure I heard correctly.

"Marry me. Marry me. Let's move on from everything that's happened. I want you to marry me."

"Okay," I whispered, knowing in my heart that we deserved each other. "Okay." I hung up then as Brad had returned from the bathroom and hid my phone in my night table drawer. "Make love to me, Brad." I reached up and pulled him down towards me. "Make love to me." I reached down to his boxers and squeezed his cock. He was right, I needed to feel him inside of me one last time. I needed to fuck the man I loved before I married the man I didn't.

Here's the thing: I wasn't pregnant before that night. I looked at the test the next day and I'd read it wrong. I got pregnant that night. I had my love child. I know as sure as the sun shines that Brad is the father of my child. Though that's one secret I'll keep with me for the rest of my life.

My husband has no idea. Absolutely no idea. And I plan on keeping it that way. The only problem would be if Brad found out, but that's a story for another time. Because he did find out and he wasn't about to let it go.

CHAPTER THIRTEEN

Have you ever had that moment? The moment where you look back at your life and think, "Oh shit, what have I been doing with my life?" I'm X years old and I feel like I've wasted the last ten years of my life. That's how I felt the night that Brad came over. When he undressed me and threw me down on the bed, all I could think about was how right it felt to be with him. I nearly changed my mind and gave in to him. I nearly changed my fate. I was so close to going with my small piece of a heart. I was so close to saying, "Fuck it, all. Let's do this." I was so close, yet I kept my mouth shut.

Most people think that love is the be all and end all of life. When I say most people, I'm thinking of women. Men and women have two different ideas in their head. I could lie to you right now and tell you that I don't care about love. You might even believe me, but we've been through too much for me to lie right now. I do believe in love. I do want love. I am in love. My husband thinks it's with him. Ultimately I know the truth. I love things about him, but he's not the one who has my heart. Brad has my heart.

I guess you want to know why I ended up with someone else when I love Brad? My first question to you would be, has there ever been anyone in your life you've really clicked with? Someone you thought could be it? Someone you've loved so hard that even just reading this, your mind has gone to them? Is there anyone who makes you feel just a tinge of regret for how it all ended or went down? Brad's that person to me. He's my pea pod and I'm the pea. Only I'm with another pea pod now. It's almost the same, but it's still different enough. Now, I should tell you my husband's name. I'm sure you're dying to know. Well, you wouldn't be the only one to be shocked to know that Dominic is now my husband. Though I suppose you want to know how we got to this place.

It's almost ironic that Dominic and I got back together. I still detested him, but I hated myself more than I hated him. I took his call because I didn't want to let myself think of Brad. I didn't want to let myself think that I had a chance with him, even though he wanted to be with me or so he said. The romantic in me wanted to be with Brad. I felt like we were made for each other, but our love story was like Romeo and Juliet. We could never actually be together. It didn't matter that we were soul mates. I hated him with every fiber of my being. Brad made me feel like I was safe. He made me feel like I was understood. He made me feel like I didn't have to have my guard up. And that was why I couldn't be with him. I couldn't afford to let my guard down. I couldn't afford to trust and love him with all of myself. That's not how life worked. There was no one you could trust more than yourself. I knew that. I grew up with that. It was a part of my brain.

Before I tell you about Dominic, I need for you to understand. I need you to get me. I need you to see that underneath it all, I'm not evil or cold. I'm just confused and scared. I need to tell you why.

Why I don't believe in love

My grandmother was the closest person to me in the first 12 years of my life. She was sweet and cuddly and all those things that grandmas should be. Until I turned seven. When I turned seven, everything changed. I can remember the day clearly. I had come home from school all excited. This little boy, Jimmy, had given me a cute little note and said he liked me. Of course, I'd been beside myself. All the girls thought Jimmy was just the cutest. And when I say cutest I mean he had an adorable little face and sparkling eyes. I can't even remember what color they were now. I remember I ran into the house and pulled that note out of my bag and I gave it to my grandma with such gusto and relish. I was caught up in myself as she read it. I was so excited and couldn't wait to have her share in that with me.

"What's this, Saskia?" Her lips were thin and she gave me a look that showed me she wasn't impressed.

"It's a note, Grandma." I grinned up at her, still happy as can be. "Jimmy gave it to me."

"And who, pray tell, is Jimmy?"

"My friend." I grinned at her, seeing nothing wrong in having a friend who was a boy.

"Give him the note back and tell him you can't be friends."

"What?" I hadn't understood why she was saying that, but I had sensed that she was suddenly angry.

"Boys aren't friends with girls. They only want one thing."

"What's that, Grandma?"

"They only want to take from you." She sighed. "Everything that they can. And then they leave you.

Ain't no point being friends with boys. They will always hurt you."

"He hasn't hurt me though, Grandma."

"He will." She grabbed my hands. "Don't ever let no boy get so close to you that he can hurt you. People will talk to you about love, but it ain't real, baby girl. Men don't love no one but themselves."

"Okay." I'd walked to my room feeling confused and upset, but I never doubted what she said. Grandma was never wrong. That was the first of many conversations I'd had with my grandma about men, and her words were never far from my brain. I lived my life with her rules and I tried to never let any guy get so close that he could hurt me.

***

I'm not ashamed to say that Dominic showed up fifteen minutes after Brad left that morning. It was weird seeing him, knowing that the last time I'd seen him he had been with Jessie. It was even weirder knowing that I'd already gotten over it. I'd been more shocked than hurt. Frankly, him being with Jessie was more of a pride thing. Which is why I think I agreed to what he asked me next.

So when Dominic asked me to marry him, he didn't actually mean he wanted to marry me. Well, he did and he didn't. You see, at the time Jessie was threatening to go to the police about the shenanigans going on between her, Dominic and Aiden. Turns out she was as big a bitch as I thought. When I heard that, I wanted to call Aiden's wife and laugh in her face, but I thought that would be a bit hypocritical. I wasn't exactly in the position to be throwing stones. Dominic wanted me to be his cover. When he explained it to me, I wasn't sure what to think. I mean, it's not the most romantic thing in the world, but I'm a practical girl, I don't need romantic.

Let's be honest, what I need is money. I don't have a job, I'm not well educated, and I don't want to live in the streets or even a studio apartment in Jersey City. I want a nice, big, luxurious apartment in Manhattan and I want to be taken care of.

When Dominic showed up, I was happy to see him. There's something about a man with a handsome face that makes you forget a multitude of sins. Especially when you realize you're all alone, with no income coming in and no one else to fall back on.

"So I have something exciting to tell you." Dominic was grinning from ear to ear. It was as if he didn't know how grossed out I'd been by him. In all actuality, I couldn't even remember if I had told him. All I could think about was Brad and what had happened after I had left Dominic.

"What's that?"

"So you know how you used to hook up with my dad?"

"That's exciting?" I frowned at him. Here it comes, I thought. He's going to ask me for a threesome.

"No, of course not." He gave me a weird look. "However, he said he wants to give us a special gift."

"For what?"

"He feels bad that he fucked his son's wife." Dominic shrugged. "He's going to hand over his company to me."

"What?" My voice rose. "Are you kidding?" I looked at him in shock, not really understanding why Aiden would do all that.

"Not kidding." He grabbed ahold of me. "I'm going to be CEO, baby."

"Okay, that's great." I frowned. "But why?"

"Do you really care why?" He frowned then. "You should be happy."

"I should be happy?"

"You fucked my dad." His eyes glinted.

"You had a threesome with your dad," I shot back at him straight-faced.

"We never touched." His eyes widened in shock and I smiled sweetly.

"You're a sick fucker."

"That's to be decided." He grabbed my hands. "Though it takes one to know one."

I stared into his eyes and for one brief moment all I could think about was Brad. The Brad I could never be with. I only allowed myself to think about him for a moment, though. That part of my life was over. I needed to move on and who better than with Dominic? He was just as messed up as me. We could play dirty with each other. And if he was about to become CEO, that would make it all better.

So as you can see, I didn't get my happily ever after. I got a happy with money and a beautiful baby. I got a husband that uses the word love, but doesn't know what it means. I got to prove my grandma right. I got everything someone like me could ask for. But oh, my story doesn't end here. You see, what happened next in my life shook everything around me and caused it to collapse. Everything I thought I knew. Everything you think you know. Well, it's all wrong. It's all twisted. You see, my story goes back a lot further and a lot deeper than you knew. You see, everything in my life was about to change once again. Only this time, this time, you're going to see it from the other side.

AUTHOR'S NOTE

Thank you for reading *True Diary of That Girl.* The sequel, *True Diary of That Guy*, will be available soon.

Please join my MAILING LIST to be notified as soon as new books are released and to receive teasers (http://jscooperauthor.com/mail-list/). I also love to interact with readers on my Facebook page, so please join me here:

https://www.facebook.com/J.S.Cooperauthor. You can find links and information about all my books here: http://jscooperauthor.com/books/!

As always, I love to here from new and old fans, please feel free to email me at any time at jscooperauthor@gmail.com.

List of J. S. Cooper Books

Scarred

Healed

The Last Boyfriend

The Last Husband

Before Lucky

The Other Side of Love

Zane & Lucky's First Christmas

Guarding His Heart

Crazy Beautiful Love

The Ex Games 1, 2 and 3

The Private Club 1, 2 and 3

After the Ex Games

The Love Trials 1, 2 and 3

Finding My Prince Charming

Taming My Prince Charming

Everlasting Sin

Rhett

ABOUT THE AUTHOR

J. S. Cooper was born in London, England and moved to Florida her last year of high school. After completing law school at the University of Iowa (from the sunshine to cold) she moved to Los Angeles to work for a Literacy non profit as an Americorp Vista. She then moved to New York to study the History of Education at Columbia University and took a job at a workers rights non profit upon graduation.

She enjoys long walks on the beach (or short), hot musicians, dogs, reading (duh) and lots of drama filled TV Shows.

Made in the USA
Middletown, DE
23 November 2015